STUMBLE
DOWN THE
MOUNTAINSIDE

STUMBLE DOWN THE MOUNTAINSIDE

Ian Donnell Arbuckle

Copyright © 2006 by Ian Donnell Arbuckle
Cover design by Jeremy Bowles.

Published by Apodis Publishing Inc.
www.apodispublishing.com

ISBN: 978-0-9738047-1-3

Printed in the United States of America.

ONE
SUCK UP TIL THE END

"Burn me."

"Dad. We know—" we tried to say, but he inter-upted, like always, his voice crackling over nonsense words. It wasn't the first time he had told us, or the most coherent. We knew what he wanted. He wanted a pyre, at the top of the ridge, burning for hours, fire marshal be damned. He wanted to go out like a Viking, sailing up to Valhalla on the blazing hatred of his enemies, far above the length of their arms and curses. They couldn't reach him now.

He was a mill worker. He didn't have many enemies. We figured a bed of branches would be valiant enough. Mom stroked his black hair and whispered verses above his face. I could hear the curses she kept below the surface of her words; I hoped Dad was too deaf or addled to pick them out of the muddied mess of her rambling.

Since Grant was working hard on his PhD, the building of the pyre was passed off from Mom's down-rounded shoulders to Brat's and my strong young backs.

"Lithium," she said to startle me from my computer screen. "I need you and Brandt to hike up the ridge and pick out a spot."

"For what?" She had the smell of Dad's medication. I was being nasty but I didn't look at her so it was okay.

"Please don't."

I've been up and down that ridge so many times I could lead a tour blindfolded, steering by the sound of rattlesnakes. Not that there would be much to show off. This here's a deer trail. You can tell by the scat which looks like coffee beans. Down there's the camera that Mrs. Whitmore dropped last month when she heard the wind in the leaves and tripped over a crop of sagebrush. Here's the trash that you folks keep dropping when you get thirsty or hungry or just goddamned bored.

My social skills have always been spectacular — useless, no matter how I have tried to train or embellish them. That's why I walked at the middle of my class when I graduated high school, a little further down at college. I was a tired, apathetic whore, sitting for attention and not quite the last one left on the streets. The sun went belly down on my education. Maybe if I had tried a little harder to be noticed, I would have gotten some immediate return. A breathless call from a stunned pornographer who could remember my name. "We just aren't meant to slide into society so easily," reasoned Grant a few weeks before I finished school.

Eager to share the prostitute image, I babbled it at him. He snickered and reminded me that women of that sort either die, desperate, of starvation or from one of the adaptive STDs. Better to be a disease.

I would bother Grant on the phone every week, as Mom and Dad used to when he was an undergrad. We would talk about our present, not our sun burned past, when our parents had often said how how how proud they were of their firstborn. He was a voice and I was a voice, and that made us equal. We'd laugh about invisible girls and unsteady dreams. He'd tell me about his work, I'd tell him about my school, and I'd know that he understood much more of what I said than I did of his speak pause speak sentences.

When Dad started his treatments, our conversations drifted back in time. Together we recalled punishments that we probably deserved, like when Dad would spray us with cold water from the hose because we played too close to the burn barrel. If we sputtered in the mud he would make us rinse out our clothes on an ancient washboard until our fingers were crusted with dead skin and blood. It wasn't as bad as it looked.

So Grant was just his voice in California when Dad bit it. The Brat and I were outside playing, which is what we called hitting each other with sticks. Mom was upset that a twenty-one year old like me still went outside to play. I had told her there's nothing like God's brown Earth to put one in one's place, and the nonsense satisfied her. I had taken to nonsense to keep her from worrying, or caring, or a healthy mixture of both. She was getting beat up and ugly enough worrying over Dad.

"Dodo," he breathed. Mom bent to him and squeezed his hand, as if that would give him charge enough to speak a full sentence. "Talk to Lith'm." If she had listened hard, maybe she would have heard Brat's yelp as my stick thunked him in the ribs.

"Talk to him about what, Gar? Oh darling, what?" She followed his sinking eyelids with her head and fell against his chest. She probably pressed the last breath out of him.

That's what I imagine, anyway, while sharp bark scrapes my shoulder blades.

Mom stutter-called Brat and me inside. She poured out the news from her well of tears. I turned and said,

"Dibs on the hatchet."

Mom went up to her room and cried. Brat and I chopped kindling until our show was on. It was too late to start the trip to the summit that night. We got through fifteen minutes before Mom poked her head into the family room. She wasn't wearing her glasses. Seeing her without her glasses was like looking at a painting without its frame. The Mona Lisa wandering around aimlessly, confused but confident; you could tell by her smile. Mom's eyes looked smaller, darker than normal, less like a human's and more like a cartoon villain's. She yelled.

"Lithium!" She could make my first name sound as though it were all three. "You promised!"

"What do you want?"

"You promised your Father."

"We chopped the kindling—"

"That's not what he wanted you to do!" she shrieked.

"It's getting dark out—"

I cut myself off. She was standing still as another corner of the wall. Her throat was gulping, but gulping up. A sound halfway between whale song and a cough seemed to come from the flapping skin. Anger, I told myself; she had no words. I could think of a few.

"I will not have him in this house another minute. You and your brother do as he asked. He asked he asked a simple portion of respect and if you think it means nothing I will I will—" She had no threat. She closed her door. I could hear her closet swinging open and shut, squeaky on its metal tracks, again and again.

"C'mon," said Brat.

We lived right up against the ridge, so the sun went down early for us. Late May, only six-thirty, and already dew was dripping off of everything. I checked our pile of kindling. It was sopping wet.

"We'll have to chop some more up there." Brat went and grabbed the hatchet.

It was awkward, finding a way to carry Dad. He was beginning to stiffen, but still flopped around like half-cooked spaghetti. We built a kinda sling thing. I felt we should have had him on a palanquin, carried on the backs of four muscled warriors. Instead, he got trussed between his pimply favorite son and me, hauled like a coyote that had strayed too near the camp.

The quickest path to the summit was across the golf course, around the cliff and up the smooth rock slides. It looked like it should take hours longer than a simple straight ascent, but it didn't. Straight up meant long minutes with feet and hands jammed into cracks, deciding either to find the next foothold or turn back, defeated. I had never made it up that way.

Besides, with Dad between us, it would have been impossible.

"I wish Grant were here," grumbled Brat. "Dad wouldn't be so heavy." I nodded and sneezed, blowing out a mosquito.

"Dad would still be heavy. You just wouldn't have to carry him."

The hardest part of the climb has always been the last hundred feet or so, the first birthing thrust of the rock. It tops the rest of the slope like the plates of a stegosaurus. Brat and I tried carrying the sling up the skinny trails, but gave up when the weight made Brat slip and nearly drop the bundle over the edge. We untied it and each took an arm.

By the time we got to the top, Dad was covered in scratches from the crumbly granite and sagebrush. It was strange; a mortal latticework of wounds, but no blood. He looked like wax. When we lit the pyre he would melt instead of burn. Then we could pour him into a new mold, like God did, and be Mom's heroes.

Brat threw the hatchet at me. The hammer end thumped off my shoulder and made a spark when it hit the stone. The metal should have rung, but if it did it was swallowed whole by the deep, dead sound of the mountain. I rubbed a forming bruise and flipped Brat off.

"Why don't you chop it?"

"You're faster," he explained and started arranging Dad's arms and legs like a mummy's.

We had beaten the sun to the top. The side we had climbed was in deep, wet shadow; the opposite was still half-full of orange light. The evening line was creeping up the rocks, graceful, chaotic, nothing like the movies.

I bent my back, chopping while Brat built the thing. He scoured the ground for dead sticks and needles with which to make a pointless cushion, on top of which he laid Dad, neatly folded and peaceful. Then he took my branches and wove a short wall, like a log cabin, around the edges.

"A shame to set fire to it," I said as the sun went silver and disappeared.

"You brought the matches?" he asked.

"No."

He screwed his eyebrows down and glared. "That was your thing." He reached into his jeans pocket and pulled out a sparkler, lost a stare at it for a couple seconds. He tossed it toward the bier. It fell into the pine needles.

I hefted the hatchet and rolled it in my hand. "Get me a chunk of rock."

"Maybe if we breathe on it hard enough, it'll catch fire," he grumbled as he searched the gloom. "Mom will be looking for it, you know, and if we wait much longer, it's not even going to light. Too much dew."

"Stop worrying – actually, just shut up."

"Found one. Heads," he called. I caught the rock. My shoulder groaned. I knelt down next to Dad's right hand and started pounding on the stone with the hatchet. The rock spit off angry sparks, but not angry enough. I kept smashing. Some of the sparks went the wrong direction, landing on my jeans and sizzling out, or settling on the dead moss floor. Brat stamped on those ones.

"The day is mine!" I crowed. First a piece of Witch's Hair caught, then a small stick, then the bed of pine needles which crackled with a sound that felt as sharp and brown as the shapes they were giving up.

"Here," Brat shoved me out of the way and thrust a dry twig into the flame. It caught, and he darted around the bed, lighting at five more points. A hexagon of fire spread, spiraled, and fell in on itself, collecting under Dad's body. Smoke started to trickle out from under him like liquid that had lost its sense of gravity.

Brat was about to feed more sticks to the fire. I slapped them out of his hands.

"It's not a weenie roast."

"I want Mom to see." He wasn't crying. He just stared at me. I tried to compare myself to him; what was I like at sixteen, what did I go through that could be on par with this? If I knew myself, then I knew him: that's how brothers are. I couldn't understand why he cared so much about the flames. Whether a candle in the dark or the tail of a comet, it would mean the same to Mom. It's the end, the ash, his body broken down.

"If she can't see, she can at least smell." I backed off a few feet. Years ago, after our monthly haircuts, Grant and I had saved the trimmings to make smoke bombs. We stole two of Mom's Mason jars and filled them with matches and brown hair. Grant did his first, to show me how: he lit one match, dropped it in, and screwed the lid on tight. We had poked an air hole, enough for fuel, but not enough to let the smell out. We watched the glass fill with thick smoke; we imagined it tickling our nostrils, wrinkling our noses at each other and laughing with disgust. Then he threw it into the driveway.

It was worse than the skunks we ran over on the mountain roads. Dad hosed us down, but that wasn't enough. He made us bathe in tomato juice, but we pretended it was blood and shrieked in horror. I thought I'd never get the stink out of my eyes and mouth.

I didn't really want to. It made me almost vomit; Grant did. We laughed so hard that summer.

Dad's burning body smelled like hair and pig without seasoning, tree flesh and pine sap, and smoke. The sparkler caught. Brat jumped back, startled. A nervous laugh died halfway out his lips. Flashes of green, blue, and pink sizzled around Dad's feet. His clothes were gone.

I watched his wedding band. It began to slide off as its finger crackled away. Then it stopped, maybe fused to the bone, or whatever skin and tendon was left. It stretched, and I thought, How silly. Gravity wins now. I could see why gold was used to dye glass red. I thought it was reflecting the deep flames but instead it was putting their color to glowing shame.

A drop of molten metal fell. Even above the roar of the valkyries, I heard the sizzle, saw the tiny wisp of smoke before it was swallowed.

That was the first day of summer. Dad ruined the whole season for me. Every time I went outside, to fight with Brat, to read in the sun, to take a walk, I could only think of Dad and the heat of his fire. I stood so close that the smell started to fade into the background. My eyebrows singed. I never got cold after that.

It took hours for the thing to burn away. Once there were only coals left, Brat suggested we start back.

"Hang on," I said and started undoing my pants.

"What are you doing?"

"We don't have any water. We can't just leave it burning. This is how we put out a fire."

"Pull your pants up."

"Oh come on. I just don't want the fire chief to get Mom's case for leaving a fire hazard."

"I'm going."

He turned his back, head hanging off his neck, and stumbled away into the dark. Neither of us had thought to bring a flashlight. I stared after him until my eyes adjusted.

"Don't break anything," I mumble-yelled. My penis was getting toasted. "Nothing personal." I grinned. When the urine hit the hot ash, a thick cloud billowed straight for my nostrils. It stank even worse than Dad. I turned my head away and held my breath.

My bladder emptied quickly. I pulled up my pants. The coals were still alive, tiny waves of red humming across the larger chunks. There was a small empty space of deep black where I had peed. Feeling like I had done my part and knowing that I hadn't, I grabbed the hatchet and followed after Brat.

Somehow I made it home before he did. We had a pair of padded deck chairs on our front porch, so I sat down to wait. It wasn't long before I heard his feet brushing over the grass.

"Get lost?" I asked as he shaded into sight.

"Get lost," he replied. He wrenched the door open and slammed it shut. I heard Mom's muffled yell shortly after. I didn't want to listen to her bubbling, choked questions.

"Yes Mom, it was beautiful. No Mom, there's no danger. Yes Mom, I'll get them for you." She'd take a sleeping pill, pull the comforter up over her head and pass out until five in the morning. She hadn't been sleeping well since they sent Dad home.

I leaned my head back against the cool plastic chair and let a rush of night air into my mouth, imagining a bubble of fresh water.

This is summer. A crescendo of last year's memories built up over April and May – things that call the soft, sweat-scented breeze to mind: the punk girl singer at the festival, swiveling her hips at one-twenty; endless card games on a green table with a cloud of Jolt floating between the laughter and the incandescent light; the hum of electric golf carts muffled by the oven air and the everywhere chorus of crickets and frogs.

I went inside.

Brat was sitting in his room, just staring at the floor. Three fingers gripped the lid of Mom's pills bottle. His door was half-open, so I stared for a while, then knocked. He snapped up.

"What?"

"Just checkin."

He lifted himself off his bed. Mom yelled something, but it wasn't important. Brat brushed past me. The bottle rattled.

I leaned on the doorframe and folded my arms. My

brother had one of the messiest rooms I have ever seen. When we were younger, Dad would make me help him clean it. We'd wake up early to Dad pretending to be a trumpet right outside our doors. We'd pile all the crap in boxes and shove the boxes out into the family room. I'd always find some of my stuff as we were digging. Toys and Lego when we were younger, tame and shamefaced porn and hentai when we started into our teens. By the end of the first day, the family room was stacked with piles of things that couldn't possibly be thrown away. We would have one black trash bag full of old school papers that Brat could stand to part with. The second day, we'd vacuum, scrub, rearrange the furniture if he wanted, and put everything back in its right place.

We did that about once a year. The last time had been only a month before. The floor had already disappeared.

I looked forward to those days. I like to make things clean: dishes, bedrooms, our movie collection. I like to wake up in the morning and stare out across my blue carpet floor; it looks like an unpolluted ocean.

Brat kicked me in the back of the knee. I started to fall forward, caught myself on the doorknob.

"Out of the way."

"Mom okay?"

"Eventually. I'm going to bed."

"You want to take a shower first?"

"No. I'm tired. Go for it."

"School tomorrow?"

He shut his door, pinching my big toe. I grabbed at my foot and hopped up and down a couple times. It was like whenever Grant would take a bite of hot food; he would close his mouth and fan it with his hand. It made him feel better.

I called Gretta and told her the news. She asked if I wanted her to come over. I told her she better not. Mom wouldn't be sleeping well tonight at all, chemicals or no.

"Ha ha. When's the funeral?"

"He didn't want one."

I called Grant, next. "Hey. Mom tell you?"

"Tell me what, Lith?"

"Dad died today."

Grant started coughing. "Shit," he whispered when the gravel was out of his throat. "Don't touch him. I'm flying up." He cut the line. I set the phone back in its cradle, trying to soften the crackle of plastic on plastic so Mom wouldn't hear. I hadn't seen Grant for months. Nice surprise.

There was plenty of hot water. I let my hair hang in my eyes, braiding the streams that fell off. I found Mom's scented soap. I scrubbed hard with a washcloth, then with my fingernails.

It took me a long time to fall asleep. I felt newborn, clean in my sheets. But I smelled; my hands smelled the worst.

I didn't used to go to bed this early.

I set the dimmer switch on low – dull ache of light just enough to make me a bronze god – and pace back and forth. My feet shuffle on the open carpet; the shag tickles my soles. I start to speak, mumbling words of prayer and meditation, preaching to my reflection, glancing up every few steps and flexing my unformed biceps.

"You see, the Lord, He moves and works in ways that are mysterious to you and me, but only in the sense that we are stupid, and so the whole world is a mystery; we are ignorant of the truth, like the screening audience of a good Hitchcock movie. We don't know what the director wants us to think, so we think whatever we can. You see? This is Jesus in the way we let the world – no, no, this is Jesus in the mystery of – Jesus is the mystery of life."

I stop in the middle of a sentence, sometimes, staring at myself naked in the mirror window. The sill cuts me off at my hips.

There is a secret society of girls who live down the street, threading telescopes between the trees and spying on me in my moments of evangelistic genius. I hold my head loose at the neck, the weight of lost souls heavy on my half-lidded eyes. I mouth nonsense words; let them read their own meaning, argue over whom I just declared my undying love to.

I slide the blinds shut, not really scared of satellites, and feel proud that someone is proud of me.

Brat tossed in his bed, bumping up against the wall. My fingernails felt greasy. I held them away from my skin and fidgeted with the cold metal of the bed frame.

I had graduated from college a full month before the local schools released for the summer. It was pure victory to sleep in while Brat stormed through his morning preparations. He woke up at four in the morning. He said that was when he was at his most creative. At six, he went downstairs to pack his lunch, practice the piano, and be ready at seven to catch the bus.

The funeral was over, so he didn't have an excuse to miss school, however much he might have wanted to. I didn't know how much that was.

I used to walk home from classes when I was in high school. We lived four miles out of town at the crest of two steep grades. It took about an hour from double doors to front porch. I was always sweating heavily by the time I held one of our plastic prism cups of water to my lips. The first few times, I could still see the road pulling away from me like taffy when I closed my eyes. I had fallen off the spindle of the world and was being left behind. I tried to hold that feeling, but got used to it after only a week. It wasn't fun anymore. I just walked, sweated, and thought about clear streams with cold water and no bacteria.

I could have ridden the bus home. It would have been a good time to read. But when Grant graduated, I felt smaller, and the ride was no good. I'd slide into a brown plastic seat, up against the metal wall, prop my knees on the seat in front of me, and stare hard at each new person that shuffled onboard. If I put my head into a book world or lost my sight into the window, my barrier gaze would drop and someone would sit with me.

Dad had volunteered to drive me to school in the mornings, if I would walk home. I got a note to excuse me from Phys-Ed, since I would be doing so much walking. I thought maybe I would feel like Frodo, topping the Misty Mountains with easy grace; instead, after the thrill of exercise and of the world abandoning me wore off, I felt like Ten Boom, or Gully Foyle, or someone who promised his love he'd walk a thousand miles to be with her and cursed when she had agreed to let him.

On the last day of high school, I don't bother going to my classes. The halls are mostly empty; the other seniors have skipped, or are outside smoking pot and laughing at clouds. I don't screw my brain and I want to say good-bye to two of my teachers.

The heavy chem lab doors swing easy if you put one hand here and one hand here. Mister Jakobs is grading papers. He looks up and I feel unbalanced, a cold ice pick to the inner ear. He burned all the color out of his left eye in a lab accident. The other is pale blue and friendly.

"Grant! Oh, I'm sorry, Lithium. I do that every time, don't I?" I grin and hold out my hand to him. He stands up to shake it.

"I have enjoyed your classes, Mark."

"It's been great having you the last couple of years, Lith. What are you doing next?"

"School in Spokane. I'm thinking about biochem.

"That's great, there, sir. Good choice. An expanding field." I nod my head, still ghostly grinning as he continues. "Or diminishing," he smiles with his mustache. "Right, right. You've got a real mind, there. I'm sure you could do whatever you put it to."

"I'm giving serious thought toward flying like an eagle."

Mister Jakobs gets my humor at times when my classmates just stare. He laughs and flaps his arms like pudgy wings. Nobody's perfect. He claps my shoulder. His hands are big and meaty, stained with carbon and alchemist smells, bruised from

13

flying balls of steel from last week's physics lab, sticky from formaldehyde.

"I'll see you around," I say. It's not a lie if no one believes you. He goes back to his grading.

Brat wasn't at school for long. He took the bus home, ate lunch with Mom and me. The phone rang. I had my mouth full of grilled cheese. Brat and Mom didn't even look up from their plates. I snatched at the receiver.

"What?" I swallowed. A string of cheddar stretched down my esophagus. I coughed and –

for a second the ice doesn't melt fast enough, even lodged in my fevered throat. It's sideways, blocking my wind pipe. I make a sound by clicking my teeth together, frantic, biting so hard I fracture the enamel. Dad looks up from his book, yells wordless, and is by me in a breath.

"Hello? Hello?" It was Grant.

"Yeah," I wheezed. "What's up, Grunt?"

"I'm flying into Spokane today. I need someone to pick me up at the airport." Mom was poking a salad with her fork. Brat was tracing circles on the stained table in a spot of spilled milk.

"What time does your flight get in?"

"Six. Northwest. It's number one-oh-seven."

I scribbled the numbers on my hand in blue ink.

"Yeah, okay. I'll see you this evening."

"Is – Lith, is Mom okay?"

"She's just toying with a piece of lettuce. Studies show that she'll eventually eat it, once it stops fighting back, but my personal theory is she just likes to torture her food."

"Good," Grant mumbled. He usually got my humor even better than Mister Jakobs, even if he didn't like it.

"You don't need to come up, Grunt. We already had the pyre and all that crap."

"Oh God. You didn't burn him."

"He asked us to. What's the matter?" I added.

"I. Damn." The curse was almost swallowed by the ambient fog of the line. "I'll tell you later, Lith. I have to pack and let my advisor know I'm taking off. It's too late." I can't remember, but he might have said, Not too late.

He hung up while I was saying, "See you in a bit."

Brat had disappeared up to his room while I was on the phone. Mom was still twirling her fork through the greens.

"Grant's coming home for a few days, Mom." She nodded. "So I'll need the keys," I hinted. She dropped her fork as suddenly as a period in the middle of a sentence.

"I'll drive." She shouted it, but monotone. No emphasis; it didn't mean anything.

"No, Mom. You're on your pills."

"My sleeping pills?" She was quieter, but still flat, like a robot. "I can take Awareness."

"You told me you don't like taking nano."

"He's my son." Even quieter. Another couple of sentences, and I thought I wouldn't be able to hear her anymore. She was fading. Shocked with lightning at first, now bleeding the charge into the sound waves, floorboards, her tight fingers knotted in her hair.

"I'm your son, too," I said, hoping this would pass for logic to her brain, blocked up on whatever she was using to cope.

She started to nod, bringing her head down. It kept going until her forehead smacked on the table. Her body shook. I was afraid she was having a seizure.

"Mom!"

Her head wobbled, the intention lost somewhere between a nod and a shake. She was crying.

"You're in no condition to drive, Mom. Let me have the keys. Brandt will take care of you. He'll be here."

"He's in his room."

"Yes, he's in his room."

"Oh."

I thought about dying. When you die, you don't just

disappear. So many people want to be immortal in the memories of nations, friends, or lovers. I want to live forever. But the truth is it's nothing special to survive. Everyone leaves shavings of themselves behind. Dad left his ashes, and they blew into Mom's eyes, darkened their edges like Egyptian kohl. That's where he lives. Sometimes I think it would be better to be forgotten.

"I don't remember where I put the keys, honey. They must be in my purse."

"Can you get them, please?"

She fumbled to her feet and scraped over to the entryway. Her purse always hung right behind the door, battered from being crushed against the wall by so many hasty young boys flinging themselves into the house. She touched the seal and it whispered away as it would only for her. She looked off out the window while her hands fumbled in the dark for the clink of her key ring.

I heard her fingernail brush against it. She kept wriggling her hand around. It started to sound like "Jingle Bells" to me.

"His flight will be getting there in just a couple hours," I said. "I should hurry."

She pulled out the mess of keys and threw them to me. I found the ignition for the car and twisted it off, set the rest on the kitchen table.

"Finish your salad, Mom."

"Love," she huffed as she fell back into her chair.

"You too," I tossed over my shoulder. When I shut the door, I could hear the cricket sound of her fork rapping against the plate.

The sun has come out on the last day. For the past eleven years, school has ended in the middle of a thunderstorm. Mom or Dad used to make the day special by picking us up after classes. The sound of black tires sluicing rainwater over asphalt makes me feel free, still. I wouldn't have minded walking home in the rain.

I've done it before, when I wasn't wearing sandals.

I trudge up the first grade, flip flops slapping the baked oil and gravel road.

Cars pass every so often, humming up behind me, heading for homes out of town. If they're hunting me, they're bad at it. I get a feeling when I watch scary movies, like a black dagger is about to go into my kidney. I have to have something, anything, pressed up against the small of my back, or it's shudder after shudder until someone slaps me out of it.

I feel that when I walk home, too. Every third car holds a murderer. My legs quake when they drive past, marking me, we know where you live, you can walk but you can't hide.

Other people stare. That's almost worse. There's no reason for it. Dumb, cold fish eyes lock on me, heads swivel to keep me dead center, just because I'm more interesting than a tree. Trees don't struggle up the slope, head into the wind, gangly limbs shading eyes. The voyeurs fly at forty up the hill. Three seconds and I'm out of their sight. Some time, I'd like to walk with a mirror at my side so they can see how stupid they look with their slack-jawed, television stares.

Spokane is a three hour drive from my town. Two hours, if there aren't any cops. It was the closest big city when I was growing up, but my family hardly ever went there. All four of my grandparents all lived in the Seattle area, so if I ever wanted to go shopping at a decent store, or see one of my favorite bands play, we had to time it to coincide with a family vacation.

When it came time for me to choose a school, I decided on a state university's tiny satellite campus in Spokane. I wasn't cut out for metropolitan life. The city's concrete and dust got to be familiar, but I couldn't ever drive more than a few blocks without getting lost. I mostly walked.

The first wave of consumer nanotech hit when I was a sophomore. My friends got tired of me reminding them that Grant had had a hand in the creation of the microscopic

17

revolution, and that I, by associative principle, was pretty damn cool.

Pedro and I always walk to the store on Saturdays. We chat about love, Tolkien, and growing up. We both took Steel Muscles yesterday evening. It's a two mile walk, there and back again. Our legs don't even get tired. The bots laced through our red fibers strengthen and support us. They are designed to die in twenty-four hours.

I snapped my eyes up to the road. I wasn't paying attention to where I was going. It only took a couple minutes to drive from one end of my town to the other. Spit out on the highway, I was going thirty-five long after the sixty sign. When Grant was in high school, he ran off the road, just a little further ahead. He vomited from stress, lost control of the car, and plowed through a hundred yards of barbed wire.

Dad slams into the computer room.

"I'm disappointed in you two." He stares. I can't shut up the happy music of the racing game Brat and I are losing at. Dad turns and leaves. That's worse than getting sprayed with the hose. I hate it when he hands us a whip and doesn't even stay to watch us bleed.

"What, Dad? What is it?" Brat mouses out into the hallway. I shut off the game and follow. Dad's waiting for us.

"It's your decision. Grant needs help stringing up the new fence. You don't have to come, but I'd sure appreciate the extra hands."

Damned if we do, damned if we don't, though I'm only a freshman in high school and afraid to say "damned".

Brat is following Dad down the stairs. I hear the front door slam.

"There's nothing better or worse."

I start to run, and make it to the car before they leave. I sling myself into my seat, back-left when Mom's not here because Grant always gets the front seat, just before the engine grinds to life.

We work for the whole afternoon. I wore my inside play clothes, the ones that I can sometimes get Mom to let me wear to church. They're hopelessly profane, now: shredded by knapweed, blotted with married dirt and sweat and a few spots of blood because I don't think before I grab the fence wire.

I pound a splinter of wood down next to a pole to wedge it upright. My whole arm shivers. It feels weird when I stop hammering, as it does when I ride the lawn mower for an hour. The world seems smoother, afterwards. Or trying to walk after busting clouds on a trampoline for the afternoon. Gravity turns godly insistent.

Dad claps me heavy on the shoulder, making my arm feel normal again.

"Fine work. Ice cream?"

Grant's in the car already, sulking. He and Dad had worked at one end of the fence, straightening the wire while Brat and I set the new poles in place. I could see Dad's lips moving whenever I looked up to wipe my forehead. Brat and I talked about space ships and swimming. Grant's graduating this year and hasn't been swimming since he was fifteen.

Dad drives us to Dairy Queen.

"I'm not going in," Brat says as Dad stomps on the parking brake.

"Why not? You've earned it." Dad looks back in the rearview mirror.

"I don't feel like I've earned it."

"Do you want us to get you something?"

"No."

Inside, Dad makes us order quick, so we don't keep Brat in the hot car all by himself. I want a large Oreo Blizzard. I get a cherry cone.

The drive to Spokane was flat, long, and boring. Over holidays, when I'd drive home and back, I would spend the time thinking about my assignments: the research papers I needed to uncover, the poems I needed to analyze, the stories I needed to write. I have my best ideas in the shower and on the road; neither are ideal places for a pencil and paper. As a result, driving usually frustrates me as much as a good comedy might frustrate the Brat.

Driving to pick up Grant, though, was empty, almost fully. School was over, for good. I didn't have to force creativity pulpy through a grater and hope that beauty would filter through my revisions. I watched a scraggly tree slide past me on the left and didn't even try to compose a haiku on it.

It was just a tree
as I was just a human,
born as being grown.

The straight wheat fields eventually ran out and the city started. As I slowed down, I caught a glimpse of a bearded man with a bundle on his back, leaning into the sunlight as though the rays were hurricane wind. He paused every few steps and bent over the sidewalk. I craned my neck. He came to a stoplight abreast of me. I turned. He was wearing dark glasses and had a hand pressed up against his cheek.

He shimmered. His face slid. He pressed both hands against it. Gray market nano; he had tried to steal a celebrity's features, probably to make himself a better sell. He had gotten amateur code, though, and was paying for it. You have to take risks.

Green light. I closed my mouth and tugged on my seatbelt.

Grant's flight was delayed an hour, and I hadn't brought a book. I waited in the parking lot and played the staring game with the guards posted around the lobby. Eventually, a wash of passengers stumbled through the automatic doors. Grant stood head and neck above them all. My family has always been tall. His arm was around someone

I couldn't see until the waiting families pulled apart the solidity of the crowd.

She was blonde and clinging like a barnacle. Grant spotted me. He slid his hand across the back of her neck and down the front of her shirt. He tweaked her nipple. I heard the opening organ of a pope song I thought was long dead, fading away as she walked off to find her car. Grant approached behind a pained expression, wiping his fingers on his trouser legs.

"Who was that?"

"Hey, Lith. Just met her on the plane. We still have the station wagon?"

"Ten miles to the gallon."

"It gives me a headache."

"The windows roll down."

He grinned, then, but it was sick, like a priest defraying the shock of a dirty joke he accidentally told during the homily.

"You really burned Dad?"

Grant only had one bag. I started back to the car.

"He asked us to. You remember. After he rented Wagner's *Ring* cycle." I could hear Grant's footsteps echo through the parking garage. I had used the economy lot, an open sky asphalt field a quarter mile from the terminal.

"I thought it was a phase. Where are you parked?" Grant clutched his bag against the front of his shoulder, supporting its whole weight in splayed fingers.

"Not much further."

We had to cross a street. A line of next year's cars crunched the gravel, spraying us with delicate mud from old puddles. Eventually a little blue Volkswagen paused to let us across. I waved to the driver and shivered at her eyes in the back of my head.

Grant muttered into his feet.

"What?"

"I could have saved him."

"If you wanted to."

"If you hadn't burned him."

I hadn't bothered to lock the car. We got in. He kept his bag on his lap.

"It's good to see you again, Grunt."

"Yeah. You too, Lith."

I paid the booth and swung onto the freeway. The radio in the station wagon had died some years ago – probably exhausted and a touch suicidal from all the country western Dad used to abuse. Grant and I listened to the mumbling concrete, punctuated every so often by a hundred yards of low frequency advertisements. Businesses bought stretches of pavement on which to record brief, five-second bursts of slogan. A work crew came out and molded the blacktop into grooves, like those on a record. When a car drives over, the whole chassis rumbles a damn catchy phrase.

Grant and I had both learned to tune them out.

"Are we going straight home?" He was fidgeting with the nylon of his bag, rubbing his fingernails back and forth across it.

"We don't have to. I thought you were excited to get back."

"I was. Now I'm not. If Dad's gone –" he glanced at me again, and I nodded. "Since Dad doesn't have a body anymore, there's nothing really I can do. Mom okay?"

"Yeah. Just retreating."

"And Brandt?"

"He's fine. School's out for him now. I've been done for a while."

"Good Lord. I kinda lost track of the months." His hands now were motionless. I didn't care for his mystery. I had had a friend, a clinger, for most of high school. He wouldn't say his birthday, his past, his favorite food: he would say nothing, slap a small smile on his face, confident that the girls thought he was somehow a more worthwhile pursuit because when they asked about his life, he gave them sad eyes.

He was born on March twenty-third, had tried to kill

himself because a two-week stand dumped him, and it was a toss-up between lasagna and Easter candy. I just made him immortal. It doesn't matter. He's dead anyway.

"Are there any good clubs in Spokane?"

"A couple. You want to dance?"

"Probably not."

They hadn't opened any of the good thump clubs until I turned twenty-one, and by then I was too busy with Gretta to really take advantage of them. I knew where they were, though. My college friends, little comets that orbited past me every so often during those four years, would call me occasionally, mumble something smothered in alcohol. I'd go to pick them up, get lost in the dark, finally find them passed out on a curbside and take them home.

It wouldn't get fully dark until eight-thirty or so. It was only seven. Grant and I went out for dinner on the credit card. We both drank Weinhard's Orange Cream soda, smacking lips on nostalgia.

"You haven't found a girl yet?" I asked after our waitress had turned her back, leaving our food.

"I have found scads of them. Lying under rocks, buried with pirate treasure, out beyond the farthest star and so forth. They all seem reluctant to be claimed and liberated."

I laughed smoothly into: "How's your work going?"

"Amazingly well. Jema runs me hard, but he knows what we're going for, and knows what I can do. He hasn't thrown anything at me yet that I can't handle. And you can see the kinds of progress we're making."

He waved a hand at the restaurant's picture window. Outside, a trio of teenage girls were giggling past, communicating more in body language than they would ever be able with their crummy English. All three had D-cup breasts on stick thin bodies. I caught a flash of vibrant purple eyes when one turned to screech at her reflection in the glass.

"Accent:Body and Accent:Eyes. Not my design, of course." Grant looked sad. His eyes were half-lidded and his thumbnail was rapping on the underside of the table.

"Shave and a haircut," I sang. Grant smiled. We sat in a trough of silence. The waitress brought the check.

"I'll get it, Lith."

"Doesn't matter," I grinned. "It all comes from the same place."

We spent the next hour sitting in the car. Grant pulled a book out of his pack and read. I yawned and watched the chaos of Spokane Falls. Stretched out on the car's work-warm hood, I waited for the sun to go down.

The intercom buzzes. Grant and I found them in the barn when we were digging for planks to make a raft. We plugged them into our walls. When I press the call button, a sick elephant trumpets in Grant's room. If I turn the volume down, then nothing happens when he presses his. We laugh and talk at four in the morning. The sun is up. Grass feels gloriously wet and itchy in the morning dew. The aroma of life sifts up from brown roots as we scuff our flip flops through Mom's garden. "Dodo, Dodo," Dad is saying from the crack in their bedroom window. This is the smell I believe is sunshine. This is more than summer. Grant decides that we should play Lion Tamer so I'm down on all fours and now there is more of me to love the grass. I laugh when he laughs and I roll over when he tells me to. We might go for a hike today. We might lose Brat in the underbrush, cover our mouths and giggle when he slips on poison ivy and runs crying back to Mom. We abandon.

The intercom buzzer goes off. I let him talk. I can't understand; maybe it's just sleep stopping up my ears. "What?" He makes the sounds again. I mumble something else and there's a knock at my door. Grant shakes the handle open and grins, thrusting out his hand. He's holding Dad's old tape recorder. "I figured out how to play it backwards."

Brat and I are on the mountain, following a stream uphill, stepping over the poison ivy. He pushes a branch out of the way, lets it swing back to hit me in the face. I step on the heels of his tennis shoes. The stream sneaks out of a crack in the irrigation ditch. "I hate this place," he says.

"We going?" asked Grant with his book half open on his chest. "It's starting to get cold."

"You got too used to Los Angeles." I slid off the hood just as the rushing sound of the falls finally made it conscious to my ears. I cracked my neck and knuckles and got back behind the wheel.

We went to this place I knew called "Repeating Beats" and I left the car unlocked.

"I've got something important in my bag, Lith."

"Stick it under the seat. Mom didn't give me Igor's door keys." Parts of our station wagon were fifteen years old; the starter assembly was two; the transmission six months, paint eight years, mirrors three weeks. I had always wanted to stencil stitch-marks around the body, but Dad was against it.

"We could lock my door."

"Why bother? Thieves don't even try the door handles anymore. That's like going around to all the pop machines and pressing the coin return for quarters instead of smashing the change bin with a crowbar."

"Still. Twenty-five per cent more secure. I'd be twenty-five per cent happier." He used his science voice.

"Wish I could measure happiness. Got your wallet?"

"With about a hundred units of happiness, yeah."

"Good."

Inside, the air smelled like electrified sweat; energy pulsed through the impurities. A ring of half-moon tables covered in bottle green plastic ringed the sunken dance floor. Light and smoke clouded and stabbed each other alive in the air above the mass of flailing heads, but fragmented over bodies and melted into nothing. The floor was owned by the merrymakers.

Grant paid the cover charge for both of us. I prowled for an empty table; Grant disappeared into the glittering center of the beat. I couldn't see them, but I imagined clouds of nano swarming the dancers: pheromone fakers, pheromone inhibitors, cosmetic taggers, surveillance. Every breath was laced with technology; pulling back, it's easier now to imagine a city as a circuit board, like they did in some of those old movies, time-lapsing the cars until they looked like exaggerated electrons pulsing down copper wire. Now the metaphor started smaller and went much further.

An amphetamine toad was faced down in a puddle of beer. He had a patch on his sleeve that read: PUMP ME A BRAINSCAN. There were three Velcro pouches under the words. Two of them were empty. The third held a small capsule. I pulled it out, tapped it three times on the tabletop, cracked it open and held it to the toad's nose like smelling salts. A few seconds later, he vomited on the floor.

"You need a refill, buddy," I told him. "Or stop crystallizing."

He blinked new eyes at me.

"Fug off," he dribbled. "You wasted. I was fine. Just refilled a couple weeks ago."

I flicked his pouch. He glanced at it and squinted.

"Just trying to help, man," I said.

"Yeh."

A boy came over with a mop and a spray can. He sterilized the barf and slopped it into a grating in the floor.

"You wasted Brainscan. That's two hundred." The toad had his hand on my sleeve. Goddamn people who abuse the future, getting high and rebuilding their pleasure centers whenever they're too burned to feel, think, feel any more.

"Get off of me."

"Gimme two."

His eyes were fading somewhere around my navel. His breath floated up to me. It wasn't anything special or gruesome, just fevered. I looked around for a bouncer. There was one a few tables down, stroking the dark thigh of a black-lit girl.

I rapped Morse for S.O.S. on the tabletop. The nano triggered. The bouncer's headset flashed green a few seconds later as the bots pierced the clogged black ocean of sound waves with their high-frequency signals. He looked over at me. I nodded down at the toad, whose grip was sliding down my sleeve, almost holding my hand.

The bouncer sauntered over. His crotch was bulging, but round, as though he were wearing a codpiece.

"S'matter."

"This guy."

"Two *hunnnn*—" the toad's eyes glazed.

"I reset him. He's got a patch. Now he keeps pestering me for money."

"Right, buddy. Let's up it," the bouncer said half with the clap on the toad's shoulder. As they left, the bouncer gave me a look that I invented words for. "Glad you're such a nancy it means more slit for me and compared to you I'm Ulysses with twenty years of lust inside my pants and a dick to match."

I sat down. Songs don't ever end in a thump club. The beat gives birth to a child that grows, throbbing its heart alongside its parent, and together they sodomize a third, and the third is an angel that pushes hopeful lovers into each others' skin then shakes the world with its groaning growing up, killing its parents and birthing a bright new generation.

Same at the Mongolian grills that cover summer with the smell of savored meat. The cooking plate never wants for food. One cook runs off his shift, another's there to orbit in his place. So many of us never quite give up.

Gretta is beautiful in her fishnets and thigh boots. She bought them with a devil in each eye but never sets her sex outside my room.

A girl sat down across from me. I could see the veins in her hands. She left them open on the tabletop, cooling her blood.

"Sorry. You looked like someone I knew," she muttered. I didn't answer. She was blonde and bright. She had painted swirls under her eyes in chameleon glitter. Her lips looked like a kiss already, and were wet. Her eyes glowed like a cat's.

"Can – May I buy you a drink?" I put my elbows on

the table and leaned a little.

"I'm already pretty drunk," she whispers in my ear, because it's too loud around us but she doesn't want to scream my hearing to death when she's this close and smells this good. "Sure," she added. "Just beer." I caught the next boy as he hurried by behind his mop and made our order, paying with the credit card.

"Do you live in Spokane?" She put up a finger to stall me. With long green nails, she pulled on both her earlobes three times. She pointed at me with her thumbs, Go ahead.

"I said, do you live in Spokane?" She shook her head. "What's your name?"

"Maria." I leaned further so I wouldn't miss a word.

"Do you like the music?"

She shook her head and almost made a face. "I'm more into post stuff. A friend brought me here. She wanted to dress me up."

"But you've got Ears?"

"Temporary."

I bet she usually dressed in button down shirts and knee-length skirts, swaying in stadium coffee huts to any music man's reinvention of the world. The bright green stewardess suit fit her much better, too small over her up-thrust breasts, her spray-on radiance.

"Where's your friend?"

"She's out on the floor."

We both watched the solid ghosts dancing in between lightning flashes from the strobe light. Their movements were like a ritual, summoning something as weighty as a Love-craftian god to annihilate the world. The night needed sacrifice and the night needed whores.

Grant had his mouth open. I could see sparkles of sweat leaping from his hair and jaw. His left hand was on a shorter man's head, his right arm around and in the waist of a girl whose hair was pale in the ultra-violet.

"That's my brother."

"It's okay. She likes that."

"That's your friend?" She nodded; her eyes didn't move. I watched Grant's hands as they spasmed to the beat. It was hot. Mom, don't be jealous, I'm sure this is how he grieves. I dare you to find two people in this place who aren't trying to beat the real world out beyond the ring of lights. I dare you to set foot in here.

I vaulted over the railing that separated the tables from the dance floor. Some guy with glowing teeth gave me the devil horns sign. I fought my way to Grant and slid a hand onto his shoulder. His back was to me. My fingernails were a luminous red. He looked as if he were having a seizure.

Maria's friend turned to me. A giggle grin cracked her lips. She made words, but I couldn't hear them. I think I saw her mouth form "twins" as she pointed to Grant and me. Her irises glowed like a cat's.

Dancers pounded the air; I stood like a strip of nickel at the center of a battery. Grant wasn't paying me any attention, so I squeezed his neck, right at the pressure points he had showed me on the school bus when I was in third grade and he was in sixth. His fist came back and shot me in the chest. He turned around.

"Time to go," I whispered, exaggerating the movements of my mouth. He scowled and shook his head. I pointed back to my table, where Maria was sipping beer through a flavored straw. A strobe light caught her, flashing her image onto the back of my retinas, and Grant's. He lost his intensity. He turned to Maria's friend. She noticed and pulled up at the hem of her flak-white skirt. Her legs, her skin, we had seen them before. They come from a plastic bubble, a pill.

Grant hadn't loosened his fist, yet. He punched me again, but I couldn't blame him. We fought off the floor and out the door, passing the bouncer; I smelled a woman in his sweat; he looked between me and Maria, sitting at the table by herself. The night opened up and let me in.

It took a while for my ears to adjust. I just stood there while the dark sound of Grant kicking a trash can crescendoed.

"Damn it, damn it, damn it," he was shouting, or not.

"Come on." We got in the car. It stirred but didn't want to start. I tried to pump the gas without rhythm. *Thump thump*, the engine caught. We escaped, trailing little puddles of phosphor.

Eventually, the highway roar was as loud as it could be. I yawned to pop my ears. Grant was up against the window; his forehead was smacking against the glass every time our outdated shocks got us over a bump in the low-priority road. I wondered how long it would take for the random thumps to form coherent sentences in Morse. A hundred thousand miles; that's a long way to drive for nothing better than Shakespeare.

After class, I stretch out my hand to brush her powder blue shoulder. She never sits in the same place twice. Always takes forever to gather up her stuff. Three pens, palmtop, paper, textbooks, water bottle, flip flops, hair twisty. I have to move very slowly.

"*Gretta?*"

"*Hmm?*"

Her hair sifts across her shoulder when she turns. Silent out here, but down at the molecules I bet the strands smash together with the heartbeat joy of the best percussionists.

"*I wondered if you'd like to study for the final with me.*"

Spring is the worst time to start a relationship. Her tummy is smooth and flat and just barely tanned. She's showing off the stud in her navel. If I stare, she'll be offended. If I don't, I have to look in her eyes. One more week, and then summer calls us home. She lives on the other side of the state, has a steady job there.

"*Lithium, right?*"

"*Yeah, that's me.*"

"*What a strange name.*"

30

"You get used to it."

"Some of the girls on my hall have a study group set up. We're doing Othello tonight, Merchant on Saturday. I'm sure they wouldn't mind it if you come over."

"You're too kind."

And she looks like the horizon walking home.

Caffeine brings my best jokes; a new audience revives the most wilted jags of wit. The club rings pretzel-legged around me and laughs when Desdemona loses her handkerchief with my voice, and Iago sounds like Disney's old bird, and Shylock coughs through every other sentence, shucking up an ugly green glob just once. Gretta's lounge smells like girl hair and warm soap, lemon, lotion, and chives. Each smell distinct despite the soup it hangs its life in.

Before I go, I ask her to come with me to the theater. We'll watch the worst movie we can find. She sounds delighted. She smiles. There was an old porn mag I found at a friend's house. The babes of Sweden cover shoot. Gashes of bright teeth and raspberry lips. Their chins are soft points. Breasts hang loose and spiked with eraser head nipples, natural. No American woman looks like that without dishonesty.

Our skins and hairs are darker and we smell funny. She had a great time. She smiles. I wave goodbye. I forgot my key.

She called this morning before I was awake to ask if she should dress up for our date. I said I'd love to see her in her finery, which made her giggle and describe her senior prom. I said I'd wear a suit, but damn it all if I have to wear a tie. She called it a handle, and her accent slips the knot around my neck.

My feet bounce heel-and-toe-and-toe-toe-heel on her thinly carpeted floor. She's in the bathroom, shared with all the other girls. They keep whistling through the walls and saying things to her in a tone of voice that carries meaning, but no words, to my ears. Her room is quiet; the seven of her hall mates' stereos blotted by the fiber weight door. I check myself in her mirror. I look normal, but with a suit and my thrift store green tie. Like a poor celebrity nude, head chopped off and photoshopped onto someone else's long forgotten body.

The clock says six-thirty and the tickets say seven. She knocks on the door. "Come on in." She likes the attention and nothing I could say could break her heart tonight.

Waiting on my bed, I want to fall asleep. I don't have narcolepsy, but I wish I did, or something else that makes you take a pill when you wake up, to keep you normal, to keep you sane, to show to all your friends as, one by one, you let them into your circle of confidence.

The phone rings.

"I'm still moving home with you, but I've got to live by myself and find a job. I'm not going to touch you there anymore, and you shouldn't rub my back. Please make me laugh when I need it. Bye," she whispers for two years.

"I love" it when you forget yourself and stumble on a big mistake. You dance like a moron and you sing like a bee. You stand in front of the audience and they laugh at you. Your guitar breaks a string and it falls out of your sweaty fingers. You didn't buy a strap. The lights go off and the curtain dries up and its time to go home. Spring is the best time to get dumped by the woman you love. Sing, Am I alone in here.

"You're slouching," Grant mumbled. "Three hours like that. Your back's got to be sore."

We rumbled over Grand Coulee Dam, snaked down its profile.

"Two hours. No cops. I'm fine." Our heads were level.

I pulled into the driveway twenty eight minutes to midnight. Killed the headlights because they mirror off of everything in the house and would wake Mom up. I know this stretch of dirt by heart; there's not a bump I don't recognize, guiding the car into the garage.

"Grant." I was leaning on the hood, waiting for him

to get his bag. He had the door pushed partway open. It swung closed on his foot.

"Mother. What?"

"Good to have you home."

He squinted around the garage in the painfully dim light of the car's dome lamp.

"It's bigger than I remembered."

I hugged him. The bottom warmth of my ear touched the top of his. He thumped my back.

"It's way past my bedtime. Wanna unlock the door?"

"Don't you have your house key?"

"Dad took it back when I moved out."

If Mom heard us come in, at least she rolled over and tried to go back to sleep. I didn't hear her until morning. I didn't sleep until morning.

When the moon was starting to set, I heard a strange hum outside. My room was on the second storey. I slept with the glass slid open and the broken screen balanced in place. Coyotes and frogs were the usual backdrop of off-white noise, like screams from very far away; but there was something else. I stuck my head up.

Grant was on the grass, crouched low as if in prayer. He was making the sound, a hum, like singing with his mouth closed. I tried to yell his name, but it had been too long since I last spoke, and my vocal cords were cloaked with mucus. All I got was a croak and a cough.

Something was flashing in the air. Somethings. The air was sparkling. When we were younger, we had gone to Georgia for a vacation one summer. Fireflies were singeing the air. I caught a dozen. Grant caught fourteen. Brat sat by the big maple in the back yard and dug a hole in the mud with a twig.

Fireflies don't survive this far North, this dry. Grant was standing, stamping his feet. I could see a shadow that was his mouth, pulled into a grimace by concentration and the sad stab of the downstairs reading lamp through the window.

I twisted my head, peered to the sides. The lights

were all around, and Grant's chanting was getting even louder. He would wake Mom up. Brat's window slid open, then closed. I heard the lock catch.

The fireflies died. Grant stepped out of sight. A few minutes later I heard him padding up the stairs, finding the edges of the joists that wouldn't creak.

With the moon reflecting its light past my screwed shut eyes, I fell asleep.

Brat slept in all the way until seven o'clock. His computer was up against the wall between his room and mine. I could hear the deaths of demons screeching through the sheet rock. I might have dreamed it. My clock said noon when my bladder finally forced me out of bed. I peed, trying to fill the whole surface of the toilet with bubbles. I couldn't smell anything cooking, but the wet scent of dish soap was bubbling up from the kitchen.

I stomped down the stairs.

"Morning, kiddo. I made pancakes." Mom nodded to the plate at the middle of the table. The four pancakes on it were dried and flat.

"Thanks. You're looking better today."

Grant was at the other end of the table, both his palms and his eyes on its surface.

"Morning, Grunt."

"Morning."

"I am better, Lithium," smiled Mom. "I had a nice talk with your brother this morning."

"Anything serious? Am I dying?" Grant's eyes were at the same down angle as when I had found out he had sabotaged my science fair project in sixth grade. "I know. I've got cancer. I want you to burn me. Burn me!" I fell into my usual seat to the first four bars of *Ride of the Valkyries* grating from my throat. "We got cereal? Kill the wabbit."

"Strange coincidences, Lith," shrugged Grant, finally meeting me halfway with a sick smile.

"What do you mean?"

"I gave Mom something this morning."

"Ah yes. Something. Good choice. What the hell were you doing outside last night?"

"She won't die now."

"She better." Mom smiled at me.

"Of anything natural. The lab finished testing it last week. I stole some to bring up to Dad."

"He was already dead."

"We mapped him last year. I could have brought him back."

I was very hungry. "Mom? What did you take?"

"It doesn't have a name yet, honey. It's still experimental."

"I told you, Mom: it's not experimental. It works perfectly. Get cut, the latent nano patch you up. Get shot, they surround the bullet and move it to the bowels, repairing the damage on the way. Get poisoned, the nano will recognize and neutralize it."

"I could chop her head off."

"No, Lith. It wouldn't do. Someone puts the severed ends together, and the nano will reattach. They remember."

I went to get a bowl of oatmeal. I kicked open the lazy Susan, fidgeted around with it, bent down and slid my hands back and forth across the rough plastic. It swung closed on my finger, denting my fingernail.

"Sunuva. You brought enough for everyone?"

"No. I couldn't get that much away."

"Great. Thank God for technology. Why didn't you tell us about this sooner?"

"It was confidential. It is, I mean. We can't tell anyone."

"They let you walk away with this?"

"No." He stared at me, probably because he had read that staring at the person you're talking to lets him know you're more serious than dead. "You can't tell them I took it."

"Do my chores for a month." I put some water on to boil. I paced across the linoleum. Each square exactly half the size of my feet. "What were you doing outside last night?"

"Maybe saving your life." He looked ashamed. It was a smell around him, making his eyes water. "It's a net. It keeps out all the nano we don't want."

"Right." I stepped in patterns, hexagons, setting my toes at forty-fives to the intersecting lines. "So, no more waking up with our eyes decorated in a variety of charming pastels and do-me slut colors? You prick. I was enjoying that."

Mom leaned against the counter, her arms folded. She was wearing her glasses, but they were slid half down her nose.

"Lith, honey, there was nothing he could do. Dad was already gone."

"You have my sympathies."

My water wasn't boiling. I stirred some salt in and watched it dissolve. The waves sliding up through the air felt almost cool on my forehead and cheeks. I heard Grant's footsteps – he walked like a marionette, dangling from his shoulders, as though it's pure coincidence, or brilliant craftsmanship, that his feet even reach the ground.

He was probably giving Mom a hug. Dad died only days ago. Mom was immortal, so now he kinda was, too. He'd live forever in her grief. Her grief was behind the pride her eyes shone, only a mirror for Grant's brilliance.

"Did you bring Dad along?"

I heard the slough of fabric behind me.

"What?"

"The meme-map you took of Dad. Did you bring it back?"

"Yeah. I thought there might be something salvage-able. Brandt's up there looking right now."

"You're not going to find anything."

The first bubbles were heating their way to the surface. The salt was invisible.

"I know."

Mom slaps me to get me to stop crying. We put him in a

toilet paper tube, or maybe it was a Lego box, and kicked dirt overtop so he could fertilize her flowers. Stupid gerbil jumped off of my shoulder. Couldn't catch him before he hit the ground. I come back outside later to consecrate the grave with deadly salt water and shove a little stick in to mark the place. I can't figure out how to twine two together to make a cross.

"We really ought to test it, Mom."

"I know, honey. I just don't want it to hurt unless it's necessary." She giggled in her nose. "I've got all the proof I need already." A patting sound.

"Mom," he began.

"Listen to yourself," she interrupted to get the admiration out. I tapped my toe. "I suppose we'd better," she finished.

I stirred in the oatmeal, turned the heat down. Mom scraped a chair out from the table. I heard her sit.

"Lith? Could you bring a knife?"

"Hang on a sec."

A little more salt into the pot. I left the spoon in and turned to grab a paring knife from the rack on the counter. One of the ones with serrated edges. A small piece of apple looked like it had been flash-fried onto the surface by our dishwasher. The steam-water tap couldn't get it off. I took the knife into the kitchen and tossed it at Grant. He dodged and caught it, purely from robot reflex.

"Christ!"

"Nice catch."

"I said I didn't have enough for everyone. Be careful."

I went back to the kitchen, poking through cupboards for something else to add into my breakfast: chocolate chips, red hots, sprinkles, cinnamon, anything. We were out of everything except cloves. Some local company used to make clove chewing gum. Clove and blackjack. They went bankrupt when I turned seven. I had forgotten about them until now.

Mom inhaled loudly.

"Sorry," said Grant.

The cloves went into the pot. I cranked the heat down and took the pot over to the table, snatching a serving spoon on my way. Mom had her arm stretched out on the fake wood surface, her mouth slack and filling with saliva.

"It's the second-most advanced piece of nano in the world, Mom."

Her arm was bare and flawless, except for the wrinkles.

"Looks nice." I dug into my breakfast with gulping mouthfuls, searing the dry morning soreness off my throat.

"What's the first?" asked Mom, then closed her lips and swallowed. "Look, Lithium. There's no blood."

"The net I put around the house."

"Wha you fway uff?" I asked, fanning my open mouth.

"Terror."

I winced and sucked cool air between my teeth. "Nothing to fear but terrorists themselves. Buddha said that, right?"

"Look, honey."

"Something like that, yeah. Nobody's developed nano that physically attacks another person, yet. Not in our lab, at least. I heard something about military development, but I don't know. There aren't any commercially available screening systems, ways to purge latent programs or destroy incoming. This is what may end up being available. The nano are constantly on patrol and can identify between a preset catalog of acceptable programs and all the rest. They don't interfere with the former, and torch the latter, which is probably the lion's share anyway. We breathe the stuff all the time. It wouldn't take much."

"We know. The world knows. We've seen the movies."

"No, no." His hair was greasy and split, jutting between his fingers. "Double-dee girls, nighteyes, celebrity sales, those two at the club. We're willing to risk it for all that."

I remembered back at Repeating Beats, his brown irises ponging between the two girls. They looked the same, stamped out of Barbie doll molds. He had never wanted me to date a bottle-blonde.

"You're paranoid, honey."

"I'm a PhD, Mom."

"Almost," I said. I had made too much nasty oatmeal. The rest went into the compost bucket we kept next to the sink, stinking up the kitchen.

"When's Brat coming back?"

"Oh, you know."

He often spent hours on the mountain. I spied on him with our telescope once. He was about halfway up, his back against a dead pine. His shirt was off and he was reading. A book was open, I mean. His eyes were somewhere else, I could tell by the tilt of his head.

"I'm gonna go find him."

"Take some water, kiddo."

"Yeah. Glad you're feeling better, Mom." Her shoulder leaned up into the soft pat I gave. She turned her head and smiled.

Damn golfers. I remember sitting in my room, playing games on my computer, or doing something small and illegal, summertime, window all the way aside, sucking with my cheeks to get the air moving; suddenly, a barrage of filth from a white-panted guy whose ball belonged more to chaos than intention, fancy that. Every day, this happened. Golfing is the least relaxing sport, to watch or play. Living next to the course for my whole life up to now, I developed a deep-seed distaste for their frustrations and for yelling at me to get out of my own yard because I might be hit by their balls.

I circled the sixth green, coming around the water trap and splashing at a duck. We had blazed a hundred trails up the mountainside in our years of games and day hikes. A few we used more than others, though, for their scenery or for skirting the worst grass seeds and knapweed.

The soft whir of an electric golf cart crept up behind me. I ignored it.

"Get off the course, kid."

I flipped the driver off behind my back. I was walking in the weeds, not on the carefully groomed grass.

"You could get hit and sue. Ain't a good idea."

My head snapped forward and back. I kissed the ground.

"Whiplash! My lawyer's card is in my wallet," I just barely managed through all the pain.

The cart hissed away. Below the motor was the sound of grumbling; above, I was laughing. I dusted off my hands and knees and went for Brat's favorite path. He liked the one with the fewest switchbacks, threading straight between the low, short trees. About a quarter of the way up the ridge was a tiny gash of a valley, a stagnant shock of muddy water giving a home to a love of green grass, bushes, and mosquitoes. You couldn't see down into that valley from our house.

I was hiking with my head down, stamping on thistles. I didn't see Brat until he called my head up.

"Lith. Hey."

He was standing on the lip of the valley. I pawed my way up to him. I had brought Gretta up here once, after, trying to kiss her. It was a good place to sit. The road to our house seemed to stretch an arm's-length long. The mountain steepened the further it got from the path, eventually falling away completely into the stiff jut of a granite cliff. Brat squatted and I sat down next to him.

"Makes me want a hang-glider," he said, planing his hand and soaring it across the golf course.

"Makes me want a cherry bomb," I replied, throwing nothing down to the sixth green and mister white-pants.

We were quiet. A fish jumped in the water trap.

"Find anything?"

"Dunno. Haven't gone up yet. I'll just say no."

"Yeah."

"Lith?"

"Yeah."

"Who was it said that sufficiently advanced technology is indistinguishable from magic?"

"One of Grunt's writers. Clarke?"

"That sounds right."

His legs were dangling over the edge. The *skritch skritch* of his heels against the hard moss syncopated with his words.

"The church is upset with how much magic is part of our culture."

"Yeah, well, we don't need God for healing anymore, I guess. You thinking about Mom?"

"Mm."

He didn't look right. Brothers know these things. No, that's lame: everybody knows these things. His head was held down at an angle that caught blessings from Heaven and slid them off into the dirt.

"She protects us," he said.

"God's a woman?"

"Mom." His chest bounced in and out with a stuttering, nasal laugh.

"What's wrong?"

"We should go back down."

His left hand had been down at his side. I couldn't see it. He swung it up and pelted me with a clump of pine needles.

"Bastard."

"Race you down?"

I nodded and he made to slide off the rocks. Forward, over the cliff. I reached for him. He pivoted, twisting down from his perch and letting his inertia land him safely on the grass.

"God. Don't do that."

Yellowstone is beautiful in May, I hear; slightly less so in June. Still, the dead sights, the stones and water, never change. The

41

Grand Canyon of Yellowstone is filled to the brim with the sounds of rushing water and wind. I clutch Gretta's camera, glad I didn't wear a hat. One more thing to worry about, aside from the four feet, hers and mine, and the three feet to the edge. The park trusts us not to make fools and suicides of ourselves. I can't help it.

This close to the edge, I am flowing with warm liquid fear. Not for falling, but for knowing that, without anyone's help, I could throw myself over the edge, and I don't know if I will or won't.

Gretta takes the camera and for a moment I think she's going to chuck it over the edge. The wind picks up. She's so light, she's going to be blown over.

"Let's get closer—" yes "Let's get closer to the edge—" no "The waterfall—" everything falls.

Brat beat me home, and locked the doors. I had to climb up to the deck and break into my own room. Grant and Mom had left a note. They were on a walk. I called Gretta.

"How are you feeling?"

"Oh, not bad, not bad." The same vocal cords that used to giggle and cry "I love you" down the line, who cares if anyone's listening in. Now her sound hovers somewhere in my chest, beating sickly wings, burned by stomach acid.

"Grant came up."

"Yeah. How long has it been since you've seen him?"

"Half an hour. Almost a year," I added when she didn't laugh like she used to. "Feel like hanging out today?"

"I've got work in twenty minutes. I'll be off at five. We could do something then."

"Watch a movie?"

"Feel like a chick flick?"

She stretches out on the futon, her legs just a bit too long. They dangle off the edge. Her head is in my lap. I can only see half. It's grinning with wide eyes. Television screens give the most

42

romantic light. I pull two locks of hair behind her ear. She doesn't notice. Her earlobe fits between my thumb and ring finger. She nuzzles into my leg. Maybe wiping her nose. She's been sick.

My roommate took his computer to a party for the weekend. We're alone with the window open, because when you put the two of us together for long, the room starts to smell like sex.

She laughs at the movie. I wasn't expecting it and jerk, startled. She smoothes her hand down my legs. "There, there, pillow man." I always jump right before I go to sleep. She laughs, but it annoys her. We're going to have to get separate beds, so I don't always wake her up. It's worse than snoring.

Sometimes I fall asleep while I'm reading. When that happens, my dreams are afraid of whatever it is I hold in my hands. Death's dark wristwatch, an aborted fetus, a pile of salt, snakes and ladders. I throw the book across the room and then wake up. Once, during finals week, she was sleeping over. I let her use my computer and went to bed, figuring I'd study in the morning. I fell asleep reading Faulkner, woke up a few minutes later when I pegged her in the face. It was hardback. She was mad, but not too mad; I didn't do it on purpose.

"No, not really," I told her.

"Well, you go to the video store, then. I'll be up around dinner time, if that's all right."

"Oh, yeah, let me just check with my Mom." Now she laughs. "Have a good time at work, Gretta. Don't get too pissed off by the customers."

"Always. Bye, honey."

"Bye."

The front door slammed, then slammed again. Grant forgot that the latch is broken and you have to twist the handle when you swing it.

Brat shuffled out of his room a moment later.

"Get lost?" he tossed as he jumped down the stairs four at a time.

"It's a good thing Mom had her key—" I heard Grant

downstairs.

"Did you find anything?" Mom.

"No." Brat. "Sorry."

"Oh, that's okay, sweetie." It's okay. I will live forever. Isn't that neat and unfair to my children who have to be buried? They'll keep a while longer. They don't smell any worse.

I went into my room and closed the door. I took a nap, straight down from gray consciousness into warm sleep, sweating in my clothes. When I woke up, Mom was humming, then the vacuum started. I breathed. My sheets smelled like dish soap, which smell like morning.

My pillow was covered in saliva. At first I thought it was blood. I rolled over, trying to find a dry spot. There wasn't one. Sometimes I have this dream where I'm brushing my teeth and the paste starts to sting, so I spit and spit and spit. I usually wake up.

I slid off the mattress and wrenched the case off the pillow.

"Welcome back to the land of the living," Mom said when she heard my feet on the stairs. She was sitting at the table, reading a novel. "Gretta called."

I looked at the clock. It was seven o'clock. Damn daylight savings time. It was still bright enough outside to be mid-afternoon even though the sun was down.

The pillowcase went into the laundry room for Mom to take care of later. Gretta's number was busy, so I tossed myself onto the couch and picked up the week's newspaper. Dad's obituary was the only one. A staff writer must have scribbled it out, since Mom hadn't been in the right presence of mind.

"Died, May twenty-third, Garfield. Survived by wife Dorothy, sons Grant, Lithium, Brandt. Much loved. The end." Someone to whom the ink was only ink, not an etching into stone of the things we can't change.

This time, Gretta answered.

"Hello?"

"Sorry, love. I fell asleep."

"That's what your Mom said. Are you doing okay?"

"Just get tired easily. You still up for doing something tonight? I haven't got a movie yet, but—"

"Actually, no. I'm just about to leave."

"Got a hot date?"

"Medium-cool, but yeah."

I meant to say, "Oh", but didn't have my mouth shaped right. It came out as a sort of "eh", with a little too much air. "What's his name?"

"You couldn't possibly pronounce it in your tongue."

I was supposed to laugh. I think I did. Silence. Behind it, the black emptiness of fiber-optic sound. I remember the silences on our old copper-run phones, how they were shot through with dirty potholes of static.

"Haha."

"Um. I have a day off tomorrow. Want to do something?"

"Yeah, sure. Give me a call, okay?"

"Okay."

"Have fun tonight, Gretta. Be pretty."

"I am. Bye."

Mom had stopped reading. She was watching me, or the phone as I set it down.

"Everything okay, guy?"

"No," I say.

"Tell me about it."

Dad smells like cut grass and gasoline. He's been mowing the lawn all day. I was supposed to help him, but I didn't, and he didn't get upset. My leg hurts at the spot. "I'm so glad God gave you to us, dear son." He's going to take me away, I can feel it in my shin, above the marrow, where you could see it if you looked hard enough. He, he, has the day off tomorrow so one of them can drive me to the hospital.

"Why do I get it all? What did you do to me?"

I know about genetics. It's not as easy to lie to me

anymore. There's a reason in my DNA, your DNA.

"My Daddy died of kidney cancer. You remember last year when I was gone so much?" I nod. "We were in his hospital room, and I was his hand. I said, 'Why, Gerald? Why?' and my Dad replied, 'Why not?' You need to be thick, dear son."

I can't sleep tonight. When I close my eyes, I feel rough, then smooth, and the patterns behind my eyes follow in backs and forths. Concentrating too long brings my brain awake, and letting them loose gives them chance to conquer me. I go back and forth. I can't sleep.

Mom and Dad's room smells like new carpet. They're never messy, like my closet that smells somehow like cat pee. They sleep in white sheets so I can see them. Both curled up like babies, backs to each other. I squirm into the space. White cliffs rise on either side of me. Warm white.

"Sometimes I just make a big deal about things," I said to Mom.

"That's not all."

I shrugged. "Anything to eat?"

"Fend for yourself."

I made a bowl of instant ravioli and took it up to Grant's room. Mom and Dad kept saying they wanted to repaint it and use the space for a storage room, but they never did. Everything was there, whenever he came home, right down to the chair he stole from the living room and we never stole back.

"Grant?" I called instead of knocking.

"Just a sec." I heard a swish. He opened the door, wearing his old bathrobe; the one he used to wear for our church's Christmas pageants before he quit going.

"What did you give Mom?"

He had been reading, getting ready for bed. He would go to sleep on the first hint of drowsiness.

"I told you. The nano repair—"

"Okay."

"She took some of her regular pills, too. She's not

taking it well."

"I thought maybe." I nodded and meant to shake my head. "You going to bed?"

"Yeah, I guess."

"See you tomorrow, then. Sweet dreams."

You too, you too. All of you have sweet dreams. I don't have sweet dreams. Not now, not under pine trees and cold when we can't manage to start a fire. I used to think I could handle prison, uncomfortable beds, even sleeping on a stone slab. I get so sleepy, I feel like lead, and feel as though I could rest anywhere and be refreshed. But when I sleep on the needles and small rocks, they're with me all night long, and I dream about sleeping on needles and small rocks and not being able to wake up and I wake up asleep.

I watched TV with the volume low, legs splayed out in front of me on the carpet. There was light under Brandt's door, but he probably had fallen asleep with it on. I wiggled my toes. My brain, six feet away, began to twirl in on itself, on the miracle that, even with the distance, it was in control. I clenched and unclenched my fists, waved at a news anchor. It was beautiful.

I heard a bottle open in Mom's bathroom, then rattle, and shut. Why not just be the way you are. It's too easy — open rattle shut — to be the way you aren't. You don't even need robots, just chemicals.

She locks the door and I can feel her eyes brush over me. The lights are off, the windows closed. The room had been airing out all day, and it smells as if spring is draped behind the canvas of male sweat and my room mate's hair gel. He's gone to a movie, and then to a girl. We're alone.

My leg muscles tighten and loosen and I shudder; it's a little cold in here. Some mornings, when I first wake up, I stretch and yawn and my whole body quakes, like my synapses are warming up to the day's use. That's how my legs feel: useless and held in lazy comfort.

Anything cold slides away as Gretta lays herself over me

wave by wave. Her skin burns and I forget my name. Our mouths are hungry for anything, jaws clenching and lips working on anything, anything. She bites my finger, hard and I press her into my chest, against my ribs. My body, something different from me, shakes.

I shook my head as Mom tossed her pills back onto her desk, rattling, everything rattling. She wouldn't be able to sleep for three hours, while the chemicals sunk through her system, twisting the brain right here and here, throwing off the balance to the side with greener grass and smarter sons. I could sleep through her watching TV. I could sleep through anything.

Dad works next to her in the garden, pulling weeds and humming talking. Their conversation has its roots in the soil, "The corn could go here," "What will we use for the bean poles?" I fill a prism glass at the kitchen sink, where the water tastes the best, and watch them through the window. When I don't wear a shirt, the summer wind makes my hair grow faster. I scratch at the twirl around my navel and suck from my drink. I fill two more and take them outside, through the sliding wire door.

"Watch for the thistles," Dad says when he notices me. He takes off his work gloves and grabs the water from me. "Thanks." He sips at his, Mom gulps at hers. "Do we need more hands, Dodo?"

"Oh, we should think about gathering lumber for the A-frames," she says.

"Yeah. Could you ask Grant to come out, Lith?"

"Sure, Dad."

She bared her teeth and cried. The sobs were harsh and snuck through closed doors like sibilance on a microphone; they flagged her grief and she should have cared. She should have stopped to dry her eyes and curl up with a good book. I rolled onto my back and listened, listened to her and to the wall between Brat and me. He wasn't moving. I wondered if his eyes were open or if he was dreaming of being on the mountain or if he slept so little that he didn't have time to dream.

Mom held a tissue to filter the whisper out. Then she stopped; the drugs kicked in or I fell asleep.

I woke up on the Fourth of July. The days had started to blur together for me. Summer loves a plateau: time filled with a very few things more exciting than sleep, meaningless words, fake anger with my brothers, movies, video games, Mom fending off the sympathy of the church and friends.

The Fourth started out with thunderclouds. I couldn't trust the first crack of my eyes, so I had to rub them and open wider. Black rolls of vapor knotted across mountaintop and valley, twisted like waves of fat, studded with platinum lines where sunlight broke almost through. I couldn't wait to light off the fireworks Brat and I had bought from the reservation. They would reach the horizon of the storm and explode, casting eerie shadows on the dark undersides. We would feel like Earthbound lightning gods, striking back at Heaven for the exile we endure.

It wasn't my fault.

TWO
SAY WHY TO FREEDOM

I pushed my nose against the mesh of my window, sucking at the air outside for a hint of falling water. I smelled metal, probably my window screen. Tugging on an undershirt and a pair of shorts, I went out on the deck. The smell got stronger. Maybe the clouds had been poured from some enormous forge and were still cooling, sending out billow of iron-scented steam.

There were usually golfers outside by now but the course was clear. Even in the worst weather, you could find one or two of them, escaping their wives or shirking their jobs, or whatever it is that makes a soggy eighteen sound like the best alternative.

I spotted a white interruption in the green-on-gray landscape. Someone had left a golf cart out on the fifth fairway. There was nobody near it. I ran to the edge of the deck, onto the porch roof, then the eight feet to the ground. My knees rang with the impact. The grass was still soaked with dew. I didn't know what time it was, but since getting out of school I hadn't woken up before nine, if you don't count the bubbling to consciousness every so often at the sound of Brat's computer.

He'd get a kick out of this, I thought. I ran through Grant's net, trying not to breathe in too many of his machines. The storm was keeping everyone inside; silence, except for the rumble, the thick clouds scraping against the top of the sky.

It was one of those hydrogen carts, the new ones that run on a chunk of aluminum. Its owners had pissed off in a hurry. As I got within a hill or two, I remembered the lengths Grant and I had gone in years past to steal one of these. Now one was just sitting there, sunk an inch into the wet grass. Opportunity is the killer of invention.

Grant pulls the trigger and a gash of paint explodes across the old man's arm. The club had been the target, but our guns were cheap. It doesn't work. Dad sprays us with the hose in October.

I hid my hands in my pockets, nothing but innocence; I was sure they glowed red through the khaki fabric.

The keys were in the ignition. A few years ago, the thing would have saved me all those walks home from town. There was some gray dust on the driver's seat. I brushed it off, figuring at least that if the owner came back, I could just say I was doing him a service, thank you sir, ahem ahem two bits guv yes of course I'm British. The dust was oily. It stuck to my fingers and smelled like ozone. I almost wanted to taste it, same as I almost want to guzzle gasoline, but wiped it on my shorts instead, leaving a long, distorted handprint.

I couldn't get it all off the black foam seat. It stuck in the valleys and cracks. I ripped a handful of leaves from an oak tree and soaked what was left with greenish dew. A wet bottom was fine to smelling like that all day. It still wouldn't all come off.

The wheel fit in the palm of my hand. I twisted it back and forth, feeling the reluctant shift of the tires underneath. Power steering. The thing was silent, even with the key clicked. I stepped on the accelerator and shot forward. The wet grass threw wings, so I flew. The speed tore up hills and greens. Thirty miles per hour is pretty fast when you can feel the wind right on your eyelids and you have to blink to keep your vision from being swallowed by the tears. I hoped Grant and Brat would see me and come out to play along.

Hunting the ninth and final hole – if you want eighteen you play it twice – I looked over my shoulder. The top of the mountain was wholly black, a part of the storm. The heat of summer died it began to rain, a steady tap-tapping on the cart's fiberglass roof.

I slowed the motor. Rain on a roof is one of my favorite sounds. It's not white, but an invisible gray.

Wrapped up in a blanket, I laugh at my joke book, but quietly. Dad's face is closed, his head is rocking as if he directs the concert of thunders and stabs of lightning. Brandt and me squinch together because the power went out. Mom fidgets and talks about old Star Trek episodes to herself. Thunder is supposed to be a roll, not a crack. Grant doesn't want to sit by the window. He said "flying glass" but glass doesn't fly.

I lose my place because the world turns white and cracks. Mom doesn't scream with Dad's hand in her shoulder.

Grant falls backwards out of the bathroom.

"I'm sorry I'm sorry I'm sorry" he holds an empty test tube that he got for his birthday last week before school was out.

"I'm sorry," he says.

"Did you see that! Did you!" Dad is standing up to make my side all cold again. He runs outside and Mom says so.

"I didn't mean to blow it up." Grant sets the test tube down. Mom twists better to the window. Dad is by the garage, pointing at the ground. A chunk is missing. He looks around, jumps behind a wall, comes back holding a piece of concrete the size of Brandt's head. He laughs and throws it at the sky and comes back inside.

"I didn't know it would happen."

"Be quiet Grant."

"Did you see it! It was the size of Lith's head!" crows my wet Dad. God soaked him with a hose.

"Dad. I blew up the toilet."

There wasn't any lightning. The day stayed dark as water. I drove the cart halfway home, then thought better about parking it in my yard, in case its owners came looking. I stopped at the edge of the course and got my feet wet slogging to the house instead.

All three of them were around the table eating breakfast. "Want to have some fun?" I asked.

"It's too early for fireworks, Lith."

"It's dark enough. But no, that's not what I meant. I found a golf cart." Grant looked out a window and nodded.

"Nice."

"Thanks. I made it myself. You're a lively bunch. What's up?"

"Seasonal affectedness disorder," mumbled Brat through his cereal.

"Without me, you're fire. I could be fire. I could burn high or be little. I could die or I could live forever," said Mom.

Grant sighed and pushed his bowl away. "Do we have any Brainscan?"

"Nope. She burned?"

"I think so."

Brat tapped his spoon against the side of his ceramic bowl. It sounded like fingernails rapping on a chalk board. My teeth cocked. I could feel it in my fingernails; even dead cells give sense.

"Let's go for a ride."

"We can't leave her like this," said Brat.

"Yeah, we can. She's catatonic. She'll be fine for half an hour."

"It's kinda cold," said Grant.

"You nancy. Put a sweater on."

"Right. What I meant was: I don't want to take a ride

in a stolen golf cart."

"The lake's out for later, I guess," said Brat.

"If there's a storm—" worried Grant.

"Let's go fishing in a metal boat with graphite rods." I shook my head and hands. "I'm finished with college, guys. Now's the time for suicide."

Brat glared at me. "I like the lake."

I have sand in my blisters. I think she was tired of my super heroes. "Try to hike around the lake a little, honey." Okay, Mom. My Mommy's the meanest Mommy in the whole wide world. She laughs a lot with her friend sipping steamy cups of tea. I usually get the carpet but not today. I'm too high now to fall off.

The sun laughs and curls up in a cloud and I'm cold. I turn back to Mom's friend's house. My feet bite. It's time to go. Our car isn't in the puddle where we parked.

"Mom?"

Mom's friend says there I am, where did I go, your Mommy's out looking for you. I'm not on the road, I'm on the lake where you told me. I hear our car's cough, like grandpa's cough. She slaps herself on the wrist and says, Sorry, on my hair.

I called Gretta. She didn't pick up the phone. She was supposed to have a day off today. Maybe she'd do something stupid with me.

"What are you gonna do today?"

Read, play video games. Grant had to get ready to go back to LA. His crisis leave was almost up. And what a crisis it was. Why don't they catch you stealing, brainchild angel. They must be worried sick. He said he'd be busy most of the day, but would be done by Fire Time. I spent a few lifeless minutes organizing our fireworks by blast radius and color, listening to Mom drift through the glossolalia of the meds she had taken that morning. She'd had another rough night, I guessed.

"Can I have the car keys, Mom?"

"Fa jo bi la my no li."

Dad strokes the back of my hand. His knuckles are furry.

"I'm here, dear son. Grant's here, too." I try to say, *"You brought him home from his game?"* but what my mouth makes of the thought is: *"I need my bubble stuff."*

"Honey?"

My body shakes and I feel still; this is funny because it's happening to someone else. "Lithium, tell me what hurts."

"That one," I point to a blanket. I hear Dad's words, I know what he means, I reply *"my head my head"* but that's not what I hear myself say.

I wondered what sort of thoughts were careening through the craters in Mom's mind; what sorts of things she could never catch with a net. Doomed to be important without being touched by the word.

"Can I have the keys?"

"Ve fo gum po kwe." She kept going until I slid the door shut behind me. I turned around to look through the glass. Her mouth wasn't moving. She dropped her gaze to her breakfast bowl and smiled because she knew something about it that no one else could possibly.

The cart was sulking guilty in the wet grass. I took off my shirt and wiped the seat down again. The smell was getting better, but I think I got some in my hair when I pulled the shirt back over my head because I stank all the way to town.

I bounced along the oil-and-gravel. No shocks, just soft inflated tires. All down my street, I was thinking of stupid things to say to the first person who asked me why I was driving a golf cart down the road.

"Oh, I'm going golfing. What? The course is the other way? Well shut my mouth stick a live badger in me trunks!"

"This isn't a golf cart. Your Mom's a golf cart."

"I'm a cheapskate."

"Sorry, I'm mute."

No one passed me, though, in either direction. I tried to remember if the Fourth was a holiday for mail workers and government jobs. There weren't any of the usual pickup trucks parked in front of the water reclamation plant down the highway.

I expected at least a handful of the dog-walkers and old ladies who fill their time between strolls with chips and cheese. I couldn't remember a time I had walked home from school when I hadn't run into at least one and had to lift my head and pant a smile and say, How do you do, I hope your dog is healthier than you.

Maybe the rapture had happened. I had always wanted to see it. A good Christian on the last level of his video game, pounding his fists on passing clouds as God tugs him to the gates, screaming, "I had three continues, you monster!" Or a husband and wife wrapped in themselves and in each other, still coupling while the air gets thin and they get cold and finally open their eyes in fright.

None of the four miles into town were exciting. The alfalfa fields were dry. Pastures kinged by rolling sprinklers glittered in a filtered green. It was more vibrant for the steel wool backdrop the clouds gave.

Nobody passed me on the road. I swerved over into England for a while, but the thrill ran out and I pulled back into the right lane.

The smell came to me at the top of the last hill before town. It was smoke, rubber on fire. It watered my eyes like the stench of burning hair, getting stronger and making my sight weaker with each few yards that slid underneath the scratching wheels of the golf cart.

I think it was my knees that hit the asphalt first. The pain raced my hands up to my head. Instinct flared like a seizure and I tucked into a roll that I wish I had on film. Waves bled off me, bloody-hell surprise and cold and not-quite-hot, and water. Thirty miles an hour speeds up outside the car.

The streaks on the pavement and through the gravel by the side of the road showed the fading imprint of my body skidding ten feet before rolling to a stone stop in a clump of sagebrush.

I woke up to "its only hold of principle aesthetic oops you made me lose my place beware of this and that and the sun okay" coming out of my own mouth. When I was fourteen, I lived a week with a friend of a friend when my parents went to a distant funeral. After the couple days of awkward individuality, we found a common greed for experience. It didn't matter much what as long as memories were made, recalled in deep midnight with giggles and did-you-remember-whens. We shocked ourselves with a trans-former heisted from his Mom's blender. We played with explosions and losing our eyebrows. We knocked ourselves unconscious. Hyperventilating, we would plug our arteries with our thumbs and bend over the bed, falling onto the sheets with red ants marching claims on all our vision. The dreams came straight from Hell, resonated in our vibrating jaws as we ground our teeth. Coming back awake, we couldn't tell if this world was the one we'd lived all our lives in, or if the dreams with snakes on bicycles and balloons filled with thumbtacks were what we'd be homesick for at three that morning when we tried to sleep.

I couldn't remember what I had dreamed. My chin trembled, shaking loose drops of blood. My voice trailed off and I put a red hand to my mouth, tasted copper.

The cart was slag. I had come around the corner and hit a tire with my two front wheels.

Ha ha. I pulled pits of sharp and dull gravel from the open sores draping my legs and arms. My clothes were ripped and stained, and weren't much to start with anyway. I could walk this last bit into town and buy a bit of aspirin at Loch's. I wasn't in bad shape; I just die easily.

Before I did, though, I thought I'd throw that tire through its owner's window. Didn't know who owned it, couldn't lift it without stringing pain across my hands. It was dusted with gray powder. I settled for rolling it off the road and kicking it into a drainage ditch.

I should have rolled it down the steep hill straight

into town. It would be something to talk about, sitting around the table eating breakfast with your family and a tire bounces across your lawn, or, better yet, through your roof. The kind of thing I'd remember it forever.

Bent sagebrush broke into dust and white flakes under my feet and in front of my hands. The hill dropped away and I could see the town. I choked and spit a wad of blood. There was fire, and there were small differences like each individual ant in an ant hill; you can't see the movement until you let your eyes drift halfway shut and let the whole break down into scrambling pieces. Then each piece carries weight. There was ash, and stalled cars, and a truck through a garage door. And there weren't any sirens.

Maybe the rapture *had* happened and I missed it. So did Mom and Grant and Brat. We were left here; I didn't have any idea how to survive. Eat, drink, and be merry, isn't that right? Bread, water, and what I do in the mornings.

I tried to keep from running down the hill; it would make me look too excited. But it's harder to walk down a hillside than to run. My toes were squished flat and foot bones bruised by the time I reached the bottom, which butted up against a lawyer's back yard. Grass bags, the bright orange Jack-o-Lantern kind, clustered around a pair of birch trees. A sliding glass door opened onto a cedar porch. It was partway pushed aside. I came closer, leaving footprints in the dewy grass. Dark powder spilled over the threshold, cut by the black spaces between the boards.

"Hello," I called. No one answered.

The next yard over had a neatly sculptured waterfall pumping through a circle track. It sounded like a hundred hands shucking corn. I stamped over a tiny footbridge holding a hand at the small of my back. The door shook against my fist, the glass panel rattling. I rang the doorbell; it didn't get any louder, even when I pounded it. I took a step back and kicked. Nothing.

My nose freezes against a cold window.

"When did they say?" I ask Grant, who is trying to do

his homework.

"Seven. Seven seven. Darn it, Lith, you've thrown me off again. Quit asking."

"They didn't come home."

In wintertime, it gets dark at four-thirty, pitch black at six. The driveway passes by the window. It doesn't make a sound and I can't see it. I might be able to.

"Come back inside. Just sit down and watch the television."

"Mom and Dad said only an hour a day. I have to."

"They're not here. You can go ahead."

"I have to."

"Fine! God." He stomps upstairs. His feet vibrate the house. When he's gone, the car should make the garage shake, as an answer. There's nothing and my nose is cold.

"Hello," I screamed.

A dog barked, startling me and making me twist my ankle. It stopped, so I screamed again. I kept screaming, like sonar, until I found it. It was tied to a tire swing, running as hard as it could until the eventual backward momentum of the swing yanked it off its feet, over and over. It snarled at me and leaped its hardest, getting its nose snuffed into the ground. I circled around the yard and undid the knot on the swing.

The dog was a black lab with huge irises. The twinges of aggression – a squint and a dart of the hollow bullet head, then a fade and a snarl – made me think of Dad. I put out my hand at twenty yards and he ignored it. Another bark, blocks away. He swung his head between me and the sound, and the more I think about it the more I think he was just triangulating. He took off. The sharp rocks must have hurt the pads in his feet, but he ran harder than I ever could.

There were other dogs and cats. I let gates open. Some came through after I had turned my back; others sat in corners, heads ruffled with dust or water from their bowls. The cats mostly fled into trees and hissed.

59

The sky over main street was lower and blacker than the rest. Cars had piled up around the stop light, rear ends and T-bones on the North/South. I peeked in the window of a crumpled sedan. Four seats were dusted gray. I tugged on the door. It opened more smoothly than I thought. The dust was the same temperature as my finger; I almost couldn't tell when it had dipped in. Thin gray and smelling funny, I brought my finger closer to my face. I gagged. I wanted to burn it off. One or two small fires had started and were spreading as much as they could with no one to worry them out.

My heart pulled left and right, tug-of-war with neither side winning. It set the pace for my legs, pumping down the drag, peering into each picture window just long enough to see past my reflection. Signs were set to OPEN and locks were bled away. There was no one inside. There weren't usually many people, even in the coffee shop, but now there was no one at all. I expected an old man in a fishnet hat with a basketball logo or a shopkeeper reading a paperback from the genre rack.

The hardware store was the last business on the road. The automatic doors bowed open for me, letting out an air-conditioned gust.

"Hello," I wondered. I stood next to the candy rack for minutes. Mom and Dad would never let me buy anything, because they were always in a rush to fix the water heater or the well or the sink. There was nothing now to stop me from seizing a pack of licorice and twisting it open. I slid a rope into my mouth and let my saliva digest it as I walked back and forth along the aisles. I found the Employees Only door and pushed through. How many times had I been in this store, and never once noticed the room back here? Shelves were lined with copper pipes. I gripped one the size of my thumb and yanked it out. It was longer than my six feet and too skinny in my palm. I let it drop. Down the rows, I found one that fit my fist perfectly.

This is where Mom had bought her new pipe cutter

when Brat had ridden over the old one on his bike. I went out into the store proper again. No one was there to ask, so it took me ten minutes to find the row with the pipe accessories. I found a cutter like the one Mom had bought. It was packaged in match molded plastic, like an action figure. I crinkled it out and hefted it on the way back to the pipes. It was titanium alloy with diamond teeth. Fourteen-ninety-five.

I slid it onto my pipe and twirled it around, biting down harder on each revolution until a section snapped off and rang on the floor. Three feet long. Duct tape made a better grip, but the smell was stickier than the adhesive. There wasn't anything I could do about that, though I tried spending a few minutes rubbing different air fresheners back and forth across the hilt.

Outside, the sky was nearly black. All the greens were vibrant, and even the dead browns looked as though they surged with a baser kind of life. I held the pipe in front of me at an angle, like one of Kurosawa's tortured heroes. Then it got heavy and I had to prop it on my shoulder half the time.

Our one stoplight was still going green and red. I swung through the alleys to avoid the wrinkled mess of cars and trucks. At any moment, a gas tank could hug a spark. With just enough air, the whole mess would swallow me.

"Just call nine one one. Cars don't explode." He has white flecks of foam from the fire extinguisher frosting his knuckles. He starts to whistle, spraying the hood with cool suffocation. "Get moving."

My imagination was burned through with pictures of heat and swirling clouds of flame. How many movies I had seen. The celluloid etched with barely changing chaos. I stood in front of the theater's red-and-black double doors. Inside, it would smell like popcorn. Out here, it could have smelled like excitement, the fumes that rise from overcooked fantasy. I saw two slices of myself. One in the angled box office window, with my left hand dangling past my hips and half inside my pocket, wilted. Almost inside me, the other stood reflected in a glass-covered coming attraction. The two mirrors were twisted away from each other. I didn't make it to infinity, but no matter where I looked, I met my eyes.

The doors were unlocked. I swung them open and wrenched my face away. The burnt ozone was stronger than before. I imagined a hundred gray piles, dirtying the red plush seats; or, with a breath of wind, clogging the air. Not even the thick smell of movie popcorn could push it away. I let the doors swing shut and backed out into the street.

Happy Independence Day. I was alone. I wished I had my music with me as a soundtrack. Something to make wide empty space feel more vulnerable. If the air was as scared as I was, I wished I could feel it. I needed help imagining.

Next to the theater was a Cactus Motel. We had never had cacti in the town, but we were a desert in terms of agriculture. Somebody had made the connection and felt a brief spurt of yellow pride. There was a pool, colored by a thin film of scum. The rooms ringed the courtyard in two stories, accented in wrought iron. Only a couple cars were parked in the lot. I tried the doors on the nicer of the two, but they were locked. It was parked in front of room zero-one-zero.

I knocked with the tip of my sword. Nothing but the scratchy emptiness of the credits rolling. A kick brought a splinter or two.

This place was too much of a dive to have installed nano locks. I went to the front desk to find the manager's keys. The door was glass and unlocked. I pushed it open with the flat of my palm, leaving grease at chest height. Behind the desk was another pile of gray. I kicked at it and coughed. There was a small rack of keys hanging by my waist. I flipped through the clinks, hating the feel of metal on my fingernails, until I found zero-one-zero.

He had been a messy man, but it was clean mess. Papers and tape, not hamburger wrappers and cigarette butts. His car was nicer than all that. I couldn't find its keys.

I tripped on the doorframe on the way back outside. I hadn't bothered to look at the car closely enough. It was a newer model, so it did have the nano locks, like Mom's purse and most of the businesses in town. It looked better with a hole through its windshield. The ignition was probably keyed the same. There would be no way to hotwire the beast without the owner's heat.

The only other car in the lot was at least ten years old. I went back inside to grab the key for the room on the ground floor, right in front of the jalopy. It was the wrong room, empty except for a Gideon Bible. On the second try, I got the key for the room directly above it.

Smoke had aged the corners of the room. The ceiling was textured like cottage cheese. I opened the drawer of the bedside table. Next to a wallet and glasses was a ring of keys. I opened the wallet and flipped through it. A couple five dollar bills and a credit card or two. I shoved it all into my pocket and grabbed the keys.

It took a few pumps to turn the engine over. Out on the road, the tailpipe backfired and I nearly lost control, throwing myself to the passenger seat. I don't know why I thought I should be scared of gun shots. My spine wriggled and I felt tired. I drove as carefully as I could past the aluminum wreckage of my golf cart and the fishtailed car whose wheel had made me crash.

Another backfire when I stopped the thing. I left my sword on the driver's seat. Someone had locked the front door, so I rang the bell. Mom came and let me in.

"How are you feeling?"

"I'm oh, don't grab don't see oop see."

"Have you seen the news this morning?"

"Oh, something's wrong with our set." Her lucidity was brittle. Her lips quaked during the silence between each word. "Grant's trying to fix it."

I went upstairs. Grant's legs scissored from behind the entertainment center.

"I can't figure it out," he grumbled through dust.

"I'm not Mom."

"Ah. Lith." He wriggled out. "We're not getting a signal. It's kinda strange. Must be a problem with the set."

"Why are we alive?"

"Uh. I got a C minus in philosophy."

"I'm serious. The rest of the world is gone. There's nothing wrong with the set. There's nobody there to broadcast. I've been down in town."

A tentacle of fear lashed around his throat. I could hear it. "What do you mean."

"It's like Jesus rode in and got lost. I stole a car."

He punched my shoulder and dug in. "Be serious."

"I can't find words. Go look for yourself."

Our eyes together tried to second guess, but I bet mine were too empty. He nearly slipped down the stairs, righting himself on the last step. I heard the front door open and slam shut just once.

I followed just enough to close the door properly and unlock it. Then I fell onto the couch and felt my throat. My glands were swollen. My body refused to relax. I stood up to watch him from the window. On the other side of the sill one of the neighborhood cats glared at me for food. Grant disappeared into the house next door. I tapped the window with a too-long fingernail; the cat followed the sound and tried to bat it with his paw.

"What's up."

"Don't go for a hike, Brat." I didn't turn around. He opened cupboards in the kitchen.

Grant was walking back with his hands cupped in front of him. The cat lit from the sill and leaped to the corner of the porch where it could keep both of us in sight. I opened the door and plugged my nose.

"Don't bring that stuff in here."

"It's Mrs. Gamble. It's what's left." He shook his fingers, sifting the gray dust between them. We would have to vacuum the welcome mat. "Tell Mom not to go outside."

"Where are you going?"

"Further."

He walked to the kitchen, and I followed with foot-falls that should have been words: I'm taller than you, damn it, don't treat me like a broken child, I can breathe with the best of them and think like the worst; I can be afraid.

Brat leaned on the fridge, drinking a glass of choco-late milk he made himself.

"What's going on?"

"Keep Mom away from windows," Grant said as he slid open the back door.

"I get half of what you find," I bravely cracked as he shut it.

"What the hell is going on?"

"There's no one left in town. We lost. Or something."

Brat set his glass down on the counter and searched my eyes for a lie. "Gone."

"All of them." I finally said: "Dead."

The milk was everywhere low. His arm swung in a violent follow through. I didn't look as he stomped up the stairs. We had thirteen stairs; I heard twenty-eight thumps. His knuckles must have hurt after.

I let my neck hang down and watched the milk pool around my feet.

The light from the bathroom wakes me up. The door makes a horrible sound when it slides into the wall, so I try to do it quietly. Brat doesn't look up. He drips into the toilet, once every three seconds.

"Are you okay?"

"It's just a bloody nose."

I take a step or two toward him, but I sleep naked. Red floats in the bowl, thick and glossy.

"Should you, um. Try to stop it."

"It's fine."

Our paper towels were getting low. It took most of what was left to stop up the milk and get it out from under the dishwasher. When I was done, Grant was still outside, but

65

not very far. He stood out in the back yard, drawing splayed fingers back and forth across the air. I cracked open the kitchen window. He heard it.

"God, I hate it when I'm right," he said.

"Bullshit." Then, "How."

He said something, but with his back to me it got lost in the grass. "Come back inside." Now he turned.

"Nothing can happen, Lith. It must all be dead now. The net—" he waved his hand again "—saved us. Just us. If we had been awake last night, we might have seen the sparks. But we were in bed with our covers over our head. I need to call Jema and see if he's all right. I—I—" He came back inside. I stood away so he could grab the phone. He dialed a long string and got nothing on the other end. Three other sets of numbers, with nothing.

"You asshole." Brat was quiet on the landing. "Why the hell did you save us?" Only thirteen shuddered steps this time, back up.

"Boys? What's happening?" called Mom from her room. Her voice quavered with two-headed fear: something was wrong in her brain, and something was unholy outside of it. I heard Brat's door pull open and his feet go down the hall to Mom's room. I think I imagined the walls vibrating ever so slightly with the sound of sobbing.

"Why am I okay?"

"It must have gone away by now. It must be safe. It doesn't matter, but it wasn't all a game. I swear."

I took the phone from his sweaty hand and wiped it on my shirt. Gray dust was getting everywhere. I dialed Gretta and let it ring.

"It's safe to go outside?" I asked.

"You made it alive, didn't you. I don't know. I can't know. Maybe it timed out. Maybe it gave up when it ran out of parameters. I have to get back to Los Angeles. I can't leave Mom here. Oh God I don't know what to do."

"I'll be right back," I said. He fell against the table and winced, the corner drilling into his kidney. He went heavy in a chair and put his face in his hands, smearing gray into his nose and eyes on accident.

"It's just carbon. I don't know what to do."

Gretta's apartment was in town. I don't know why I didn't stop by there before. It didn't cross my mind that she could be gone with all the others. I used to be envious of people in Florida for all the hurricanes they got. Natural disasters are as beautiful as they are godly. They happen to other people; people in big cities everywhere. But Gretta was one of me and that made her free. We snuck away from God, too small for him to see, and his rainbows meant nothing anymore.

The sky was still black and heavy; it had forgotten how to let the water out.

I pulled up on the lawn of Gretta's apartment building. Empty cars were scattered loosely through the drive and road. She didn't answer her buzzer. I ran back to the car and pulled my sword. I swung and shattered the glass by the entryway. The alarm had a red sound. I scraped through the hole, tearing my clothes.

Her door was double locked, but I had time. I bruised myself until it fell away. Her lights and television were on, fighting for space, blue against gold.

"Gretta?" I should have taken my shoes off, but I didn't.

She must have been getting ready for bed. Her schedule was magneted to the fridge. No work on Independence Day. I ripped the slip of paper in half and threw it away. Her bedroom door was open. "Are you in here?"

I threw back the sheets, and, in doing so, I scattered some of her around the room. She hadn't been that fat. There was more dust here than I had seen before. Two people could have made that much. The piles weren't divided.

Jealousy or not, I kicked the T.V. in.

Sweat is the center. For a moment that matters more than its brothers, a drop hangs in the nothing distance between his chest and hers. The faint iridescent skin makes him look as though he was sculpted out of stained diamond. Her gentle thrill responds. There is a shudder, and a second, and the drop hits between her breasts. It will soak into her skin or evaporate into his salt dust. She opens her eyes wider and he grins because he makes her feel like dying; but her eyes don't close again. The color that he loved so much in the amber tavern light is fading, turning gray. "It hurts it hurts dear gods it hurts take it out take it out." Just an it now. He obeys and reaches up a hand to scratch his back. It comes away on his fingers and he crumples into her chest in shock. His head keeps going in until he feels the comfortable resistance of the bed; then he stops feeling and his lips drip into dust.

I vomited, wiped my mouth with the back of my hand, wiped my hand on a clean spot of blanket and fumbled out with the stain on my mind.

A short, natty dog was waiting on the front step for me. I kicked at it, ten feet away. Its head followed my foot, but nothing else.

"Get off."

As I walked past, it attacked. I felt its centimeter teeth in my skin, tried kicking with my other foot. Balance gone, I scraped my elbows on the pavement. The dog was at my throat. I did the only thing that came to mind. I bit it. Its hair tasted like rotting pine sap but I couldn't spit. My fists got under its rib cage and pounded; I was so strong and it was so brittle. I stood up when it was dying and put a hand to my throat. Blood coursed down my leg, and jugged between my fingers. The drug store was two blocks away. I could make it.

I collapsed in the middle of the street and stayed there for a couple minutes with my head between my legs, savoring the oxygen in my brain and the incongruity of feeling healed on the busily burning main.

I had left my sword back at the apartment building. The safety glass in the drugstore's door bent and waved against my foot before it shattered and folded into a neat pile on the sidewalk. I ducked under the push bar. The lights were off. They always closed at six on weekdays.

Bandages and pills. I patched myself up as best I could and stuffed some extras in my pockets for Mom. By the magazine rack, I ducked under a wave of dizziness. When it passed, I reached for a gossip rag and read the page of loose tongues that the celebrities wagged at each other. It was getting hard to tell their words apart. You stole the shape my ears make during the act of love. You stole my husband. No that wasn't me that was my twin, my triplet, my quintuplet, your Mom.

I grabbed a handful of bars from the candy rack and munched through them, letting the cellophane wisp to the floor. They scratched over the tan squares of carpet with a sound like the clicking of a cat's claws.

When I could stand without wanting to tear out my eyes, I walked over to the toy aisle. "Buy me that, buy me that," whispered my fingers on the cardboard and plastic. I had wanted something every time Mom and I came in here to fill a prescription.

"It's not for you this time."

"Does that mean I can get a toy?"

"No, honey. In no way does that mean that you can get a toy. You can look, though, if you like."

The stuffed animals smell horrible, but I bury my face in them anyway, to comfort them. I hang from the monkey bars at school when there's no one else, but I don't like to be there forever. The toad has been up by his neck ever since I can remember. He smiles with his eyes and crooked mouth but he smells bad, like when I don't go to the bathroom for number two and try to hold it in.

"Let's go, kiddo."

"Can I take it with the eye dropper?"

"This isn't for you. It's for Brandt."

Super Morphing Heroes. Regen Soldiers. Bottle Rocket Flyers. Bloody fucking hell.

I felt a shiver in my back. It didn't stop, even with both hands pressed against my kidneys, so I sat with my spine against a wall and waited for it to pass. It moved from behind me to my ears and I realized that I could hear the high engines of a jet. I ran outside but couldn't see anything through the clouds. It was there, though just out of sight. I half expected the rain to finally be shaken out by its rumble and scream, and thought I might help.

Nothing. The sound was fading. That meant the jet itself was long gone. Were there still people alive elsewhere in the world? Was the jet just cruising, empty, on autopilot? Would it soon run out of fuel and crash into the tundra where no one would appreciate or run to help? But Grant had called Los Angeles, and there hadn't been anyone. Our town was near the hydroelectric center of the whole Northwest. Had we been a target, then? I had to get inside somewhere.

The theater was across the street, its doors unlocked. I paused with my fist around the black semi-circle handle and held my breath. It didn't matter. When I opened the door, I could still smell the aging air full of the city. I retched, but nothing came out.

The lobby was quiet and thick with carpet and butter flavoring. I had always wanted to see the projection room. I prowled around for a few minutes, ripping open the locked drawer of candy, tapping on walls. Back when the theater was built, in the 40s, it wasn't in good taste to show the patrons they were getting into anything but magic. The box-office was circled by a leaden red curtain and the door to the projection room was nowhere to be seen. I had to pee. The bathrooms were painted and repainted "Gentlemen" and "Ladies". The Ladies' room had couches. I went in there.

There was another door set in the back wall, locked. It was painted the color of the wall and was narrower than the bathroom's entrance. It had a tiny silver knob, like on a medicine cabinet. I knocked on it. My bladder tugged against my curiosity. Both won, so I went fast and left the seat up. Zipped again, I pulled hard on the thumbnail-sized handle. It came off in my hands.

"God damn." As if he'd care about a door.

The hinges were on my side of the door, ugly with paint but still accessible. There were two: one at the top and one at the bottom, jutting out with three-inch pins. I worked my thumbnail under the head of the top one and tugged until I felt my cuticle pulling away. Lord, the small things hurt. I switched hands, sucked on the pain and tugged again. The paint was cartoon skin color, but bits of metallic skeleton were starting to show through tiny cracks.

Another switch, suck, and tug and the pin budged almost an inch.

"Careful, Lith. Did I ever tell you bout the time I was carrying a fridge for my Dad and popped my nail off? Didn't even drop it or anything. Just popped off from the strain."

"Yeah, Dad."

"It grew back, though. Watch your end, there."

"I'm slipping."

"Grant! Would you mind helping out?"

"Be right there, Dad."

"Can you hold it?"

"Yeah, I got it," says Grant. It's sweating.

The first one popped out and rattled like plastic on the floor. I tried getting my fingers into a crack and tugging the door off, but it was too thick to bend. Both my knees cracked when I bent down to attack the second hinge. I switched to index fingers, back-and-forth.

I tore off half of the nail on my left hand and it bled against my tongue, but I got the pin out. I stood back and kicked at the door. It shuddered, complained and sagged back into a dark stairwell.

Squeezing through the skinny hole, I thought I heard a rat. Not the skittering fingers but a squeaking. Hungry babies begging naked and blind for milk. I let my lips close over my teeth and breathed carefully.

The steps were tall and lipped; I kept stubbing my toes. "Sunuva—" at the top was another door "—bitch—"

that was in my face and feet before I expected it to be. The handle was warm and fit fully in my fist. It wasn't locked, thank God. I sucked my finger.

A sphere-shaded incandescent bulb hung down to eye-height at the center of the room, a few feet from the massive analog projector. The woman who owned the theater was short. She only came up to my shoulder when she was standing at the snack counter. I set the pads of my right hand lightly on the lacquer black metal. The spools and bobbins were spinning. Something was clanking, deep in the maze of machine and film. The projection light was still on. I bent to peer through the window, passed my hand in front of the column of light.

"Stop whining! You knew it was hot."
"Well, Dodo, now he really knows it."

I blew on my fingers but my breath felt blazing hot, as if I was spraying oil on a fire.

I poked around the cubicle a bit, trying to find the can the film had been in. It was sitting on a desk next to a paste pot. Some things don't want to change; some people don't want them to. They form alliances. The owner with her scissors and the paste, editing the film to outmoded MPAA standards, illegal but hey who gives a damn out here.

They had been watching some children's cartoon. I don't remember the name now, and would make fun of it anyway. I bent into the window again, looked out at the dusty red luxury chairs, let my forehead sink onto the sill and cried.

It took a few hours to get everything just right, same as it would if I had been making a giant domino knock over, but it gave me something to do. I pulled the archives out and spread their guts around both bathrooms and the lobby. I kept pausing to hold a foot long strand to the light, recognizing an actor's face and situation. I pulled a set of credits from the first re-release of *Star Wars* and crammed as much as I could into my pockets. Grant once had a flipbook full of flash paper. He lit a match, let it go out, made a motion with his wrist and the whole thing almost took off his eyebrows.

"There. You see? You have to be careful with this stuff, Lith."

"Let me try."

"No, it's my birthday present. Here watch."

He takes a bit of plastic pipe and jams it full of wadded paper. In the other end, he stuffs a black rubber plug with a hole in its center.

"Where's that anthill."

I take him to it and scratch my ankle.

"Fire in the hole!"

"Hill," I say. He sticks the match through the plug and the pipe farts a flame as long as my arm.

"You're gonna burn the field!"

"It doesn't get hot enough. Look at em."

The ants are running back and forth because their sky was gone, but now its back again. I try to count them, but they're disappearing and I can't tell where one begins and another stops beginning. A few are dead, I think, but they're moving. A few are dead, but there will be more because the sky is gone again.

"You're gonna run out."

"That's what it's for."

I had to go back to the drug store for a Bic. I popped the mechanism to make a crack lighter, like Mister Jakobs had shown me in chemistry. It burned as I walked back across main street, despite the wind that was strong enough to toss sharp particles of dirt.

"I dub thee Prometheus." I threw him through the propped-open doors and ran. It sounded wet. Some things catch fast and the building was old. The film burnt away like flash paper, but it was hot enough.

"Lee-thee-oom!" I thought I had made it around the corner fast enough. I can't ever wait to see her again and let her be nice to me. I can wait, but it takes a little while to get used to it, for her

73

and for me; times are that I want her to remember the last smart thing I said, not give me the chance to be stupid again. I can't help it. She brings out the blood in me.

"How are you, Gretta-face?" Her perfume washes around a step behind her, like the train of a wedding gown.

"Fine, thanks, and how are you?"

"And how are you?" I stumble. "That leaves you one up."

"Whatcha mailing?"

"Oh, a letter to one of my old teachers. Just keeping in touch." I slide the skinny thick note through the slot in the wall with that always-catch in my heart as I convince myself I forgot the stamps.

Out of the spiked stream of winter coats and red noses, Pedro bleeds off towards us. He doesn't take notice; his head bends to his mailbox. His hair gets there first. He fiddles with his combination, ticking the numbers left and right across his eyes.

"Yeah, it's a letter asking her if Pedro's an ass."

He rubs his scalp with his middle finger. "You made me lose count."

"It's one, then two. After that comes three if you can 'member that much."

"Ah, yeah. Thanks. Bastard."

"What are you doing today?"

Pedro doesn't answer, but Gretta does, and that's what I was going for anyway.

"I've got a quiz in my sosh class. Might go ice skating tonight with some of the girls."

"Oh, that sounds like fun."

"Yeah, it'll be pleasant."

Pedro fishes a slip of brown paper out of his box. "I got a package."

"I don't even get junk mail."

"Me neither," says Gretta. "Well, I'd better go study. Good to see you, Lith. We need to hang out and chat some time."

"Yeah we do. See you later."

"Okay."

I swing into Pedro's coat-tails as he goes to collect his package. Dear diary, today I met a girl again and she smiled at me. It might have been the first time. That would never make a good story.

"What did you get?"

"You'll just have to wait and see, won't you?"

"Ass."

"Yeah, you just wait." He hands the girl at the desk his slip and ID. Her expression is frozen from sorting through the dead letters and magazines. Pedro props a gangly arm next to the register and twirls a lock of hair with his free hand.

"When are you going to cut it, tweaker?" I ask him.

"Just stop trying Delilah. Yeah that's right. Think about it."

"Here," says the post girl.

"Thank you so much."

The return label is a rotating design of molecules, chameleon colored to complement the tone of its surroundings. Right now, it's a light purple and dark green.

"What did you get?"

"Something wonderful." I made him watch Kubrick's 2001 last night, and I don't think he'll ever forgive me for it. He uses his keys to slice open the packing tape and pulls out a pop-ribbon of capsules, about twenty. I read the sticker under his thumb.

"Body:Spiderlegs? I haven't read about that one."

"It's funner than a speeding bullet, my friend."

"More fun than a speeding bullet."

"Damn you English majors and your long-ass hair." He tears off two capsules and births them into his palm. His veins are clear and red, the skin between them pale; he looks as if he has scales.

"I'll cut it when you do."

"Try this with me."

We suck them down at the water fountain. Crash in the center lounge while the mods take effect.

"You're still after Gretta?"

"Yeah. And she knows it."

"Sam gave you his blessing, you know."

"He's just one of those guys that feels better if all his friends are hooked up. They're a dangerous breed."

"We could shoot him."

"Yup. How long for this?"

"Anytime now." He starts pulling off his shoes and socks, his winter feet full of sweat. The bottoms are covered in something black. My slippers and socks follow. I run a hand along the bottom of my foot. It's hard, and kind of sticky.

"Roll up your legs, too." He pulls up his pants and fastens them above his knees. His shins are covered in the black, too. "It's like Velcro, see? You've got to be careful, but—"

He lurches to a wall and shoves himself up against it. I want to take a picture because it looks like he's urinating. Then he starts to climb.

"Damnit. I thought it did the hands, too."

"It says spider legs," I wrench, coming up next to the wall and further up next to him. "This is pretty cool, anyway." We're up six feet, now, halfway to the balcony.

"I wonder how well it works on glass."

The lounge is domed by mirrored plexi, baking us in the Spring like a magnifying glass and coaxing us in the Winter when we least expect it.

"You first," I say.

"I've got to do everything around here?"

"It's your money."

He hugs what he can against the smooth sky, but I can tell his back is breaking. Gently, he curves away so he's kneeling upside-down.

"How does it feel?"

"The blood's all rushing to my head. Aiya." He lets go a gob of spit. I hear it splash, but don't see what it hit. I'm up next to him, peering between my legs at a splotch of white cloud that looks like a flower or a starfish.

"Ugh. I'm getting nauseous," I say.

"Hey, you!" We're right outside the Student Services offices. An old angled woman glares at us.

"Yes?"

"Get down from there!"

"We're not endangering anyone," says Pedro.

"For another fifteen minutes," I add. Pedro slaps the back of my head and I almost lose my balance to a two storey fall.

"I'm sure we have a policy about this."

"You check, ma'am. We'll come down."

It's hard to get my pant legs back around my ankles. I cram the heels of both hands against my nostrils, but I can't smell anything; it's just sticky.

"This stuff is nasty."

"In the good sense or the bad sense?"

"Both. I'm going to wash my hands and then go home. I'll see you at dinner, Pedro."

"Yeah, right. Dinner." He rubs his back.

Dogs were barking and Mom was gone when I got home. The mountain was like a band shell, bouncing every canine sound – the short, airy squeals; the gravel barks – straight into the house. They were hungry, or missing their masters, and out of luck. The neighborhood dogs had always messed with our cats.

"Where'd Mom go?"

Brat was watching a movie. "Out. I saw some smoke down in the valley."

"That's because you're observant. Where'd Mom go?"

He sighed and clicked off the television with a magic

wave from the remote. "Nothing's showing on the channels, anyway. She and Grant went for a walk. Grant took the kitchen knives."

"Oh, that wasn't very thoughtful of him. What if I need to dice some carrots?"

"Ess oh ell, brother. I'm going for a hike."

"Now?"

"No. Just thought I'd tell you twenty-four hours in advance, so you could be prepared when the time does come."

"That's very thoughtful of you."

"I'm a thoughtful guy." He stood and cracked his knuckles on each other. "It's true, huh."

"About being thoughtful? No." He snorted and turned toward a window. "But. Not all that smoke was from me. God's honest truth."

"God doesn't care. I should sleep in the Gambles' house tonight."

"Yeah, if you can get the smell out."

"What smell?"

"The gray crap. It smells awful."

"Grant was messing with it. I couldn't smell any-thing."

"Did he find anything?" I asked.

"Um. I didn't want him to take the knives."

Now I was home alone. I imagined the house like a molecule; we were electrons, floating around its nucleus in a cloud of probability. Together we make a whole and we always come back, from vacation and school. We always come back.

"Mom, I want to talk to you," I said as soon as she walked in the door.

"You'll have to fend for yourself."

"No, I'm fine. I had a pizza."

"What is it, honey?"

I can't get your smile out of my head, and it's making

me go nuts. Have you looked around you at the Earth frowning and do you even get beyond the vague and learn what this means? Following Dad out of life came the rest of the world, though he was never much of a trend-setter. This whole mess just makes no sense and my words are not enough to make you stop being a clown with your grin and old clothes, Mom you're a clown and I need you to take this seriously.

"Sorry. I meant I need to talk to Grant." He had already slipped up to his room, two-at-a-time up the stairs. I knocked on the door through the poster of Columbia making its final launch. He opened it with one hand, cracking the knuckles of the other under his chin while he stared at his old computer's screen. The new one was in LA.

"Proud?"

"What?"

I punched him in the shoulder. "Are you proud?"

"What's your problem?"

"For Christ's sake, Grunt! Everyone in the world died today."

"I don't think it was the world. Maybe it was just our town and the few hundred miles around us."

"God damn it, I don't care."

"You have to keep calm."

"Or shut up."

He turned around and pushed me down hard onto his bed. His neck craned down over me and he touched his forehead to mine.

"No, don't shut up. I got an e-mail from Jema. A few of them are okay. They're looking for other survivors. We're going to be fine."

"Are they coming here?"

"I don't know. That wouldn't make any sense, though. And some of the mail systems went down, so I can't get to him again."

"So you're giving me bullshit."

"We weren't the only ones, Lith." He finally pulled

away, he and his halitosis.

"It was your net, wasn't it?"

"Yes."

"Proud?"

"No, but—"

"Yeah. But."

A bright green flash filtered through his closed blinds.

"The Brat's gotten into the fireworks."

"We may as well celebrate."

"If you say we can celebrate being alive, I'm going to pee in your underwear drawer the next time you're out."

He turned around and walked out. I heard the bathroom door open and close, and a minute later his feet pounded down the stairs.

"Brandty?"

"He's not inside Mom," I yelled. The lightning crack of a rocket provided me with a period.

"Oh. Could you get me some juice?"

"Sure."

I imagined this: Brat on one side, Grunt on the other, sparklers in hands, pawing through our bags of gunpowder lights. An acrid tail, solidified by bright yellow flashes, dusting both their faces with sulfur and shadows. I could see Grant's face, smiling back through the centuries at the lovable Chinese for making such a wonderful discovery as these bottle rockets and blasts. His heart leaping at each explosion because it's the only one. The only child.

Brat's face is stony but for his twitching nostrils when a spark stings him. He has to remember the time his friend Josh got under the path of a misfired twirler. It fell down his v-neck and spun against his chest like an angry kitten. He smelled of vitamin E for the next eight months; he screamed for the next five hours.

I got Mom her juice. Dad's rock-hard pillow was still on his side of the bed. I sat down at the foot.

"I'm so tired," said Mom.

"It's been a long day," I replied.

"What did you do, honey?"

"Not much. You don't have any scars."

She twisted first one wrist in the lamplight, then the other, switching the juice between hands.

"Not a one. It's amazing, really."

"Night, Mom."

"Good night."

Behind my own door, I cried again and didn't know why. It wasn't Gretta, just Gretta. Something else was broken, and a window was clanging open and shut with a metal frame. We don't make those anymore. I fumbled with my tears to make a pool, a mirror, and see the future but it was too thin and escaped between my fingers. Not enough, either; any way I look at it, I wasn't good enough to make sense of my life or their deaths or gray dust or a brother's love for me.

The first wave ebbed away, leaving me curled up under my melodrama. I dried my eyes off and toppled over into bed. The sheets cool and slick; I bicycled my legs slowly, just to get the feeling. It was green.

Through my pillow, the shattered sounds of powder were as soft as croaking frogs and the circle chut-chut-chut of the golf course's automatic sprinklers. I fell asleep; it wasn't even ten o'clock.

Mom got me up at six.

"Rise and shine, son of mine. We need to have a family meeting."

I had been awake for half an hour already. My dreams were rough, then soft, then rough. My pulse of instinct for survival woke me up when it got to be too much, that up and down – or more like side to side.

I rolled off my low mattress. The carpet tickled the bottoms of my feet. Friction heat is a tiny thing, but for finding my way back to open eyes it works better than coffee.

Grant sat in Dad's old spot. He had probably forgotten our seating habits since he'd been away so long. My chair was pulled out and ready for me.

"Morning, Lith."

"Go to hell, Grunt."

"Give me a map."

"Watch your mouth, Lithium," said Mom. "Come on, now."

"Breakfast?" I asked.

"Already had it," said Brat with a squeak on "had".

"Damn it."

"Lithium!"

"What?"

Grant cleared his throat and splayed his fingers across the tabletop. "Okay, come on. This is serious." This is serious. "We need to figure out what we're going to do next. We can't just stay here, I don't think. This region doesn't bring in enough food or resources."

"I like how you're so calm." He ignored me or I didn't say it out loud or at least not with those words.

"We could move into one of the cattle farms, but then we'd have to work it, and there are only the four of us."

"All we need to find is a warehouse stocked with nano," said Brat. Grant slapped him on the back of the head.

"Wake up, Brandt. The only nano we can trust is the shock I gave to Mom, and the stuff I've got left in my pack. All others could be contaminated. In fact," his face clouded. "I wouldn't be surprised if the virus built off of the architecture of the common consumer nano."

"Whoa, cowboy. You're sure it's a virus?"

"Not a biologic. A silicon. And yes, from what I can tell. The gray dust is the same as all the tests we've run in the labs."

"You found that out using the Mister Wizard Microscope Three-Thousand you left in your closet, did you?"

"I have other equipment."

"Sure."

"Unimportant. And irrelevant, Lith. What else could it be? It only attacked biological material; and what's more, it only attacked *human* biological material. That's not natural, and that's not an accident."

"So that means that whoever did that could still be around," said Brat.

"Could be, but I doubt it. It sounds like psychotic behavior. They probably didn't go in too deeply with protection countermeasures."

"Protection measures. And you got a C in Psych one-oh-one."

"Lithium, honey, please focus." She didn't want to say it, or she didn't want her voice to crack like that. "This is important."

"Yes, Mom. I'd love not to care, but I really do."

"So," said Grant, regaining control. "Mom and I are going to drive to Spokane and see what we can find there. Brandt, you and Lithium are going to stay here in case I get a call from Jema, or from anyone else for that matter." Look at us pulling toward the nucleus, losing energy, coming together probably.

"The phones are still working?"

"I don't see why they wouldn't be." He lifted the kitchen unit from its cradle. I heard the faint buzz of the dial tone. He set it back down. "And while we're gone, you guys take stock of the non-perishable foods we've got and start hoarding water. We're going to need it. Okay?"

Yeah yeah yeah. They took off for their day in the park. Mom drove. Brat hunkered down in the pantry and started throwing cans and tins into a pile on the kitchen linoleum.

"I'm gonna fill the bathtub, I guess," I said.

"Mmkay."

"You remember where we keep the Coleman jugs?"

"Yeah. They're hiding somewhere in the barn. Oh crap. Look at this." I bent for the jar he handed out. Olives, with labels from the nineties.

"Where did this stuff come from?"

"I don't know. This shelf's full of it, back behind

Mom's canned prunes."

I rolled the label around.

"This shit expired ten years ago. Probably kill us if we eat it."

"In the cosmic scheme of things, I guess that wouldn't matter much," he mumbled and crashed a double handful of the things into the compactor.

"Yeah. And it wouldn't have mattered much if Adam and Eve had come down with the sniffles and keeled over before Cain and Abel came along."

I ran cold water into the tub in Mom and Dad's bathroom. Only four inches, remember.

"But I want to swim. We never go to the pool anymore."

"You couldn't swim in this tub, anyway, Lithium. It's too short for you."

"Or I'm getting too big for it, right Dad?"

"That's right. So we don't want to waste water. When it gets to here—" he taps his first row of knuckles and stretches out his fingers *"—then turn the water off, okay?"*

"Okay, Daddy."

"Make sure you keep splashing so one of us can hear you, okay?"

"Okay, Daddy."

"We wouldn't want to lose you, now, okay?"

Okay, sir. Respect should gloss your eyes because experience shines. You're older than I'll ever be, and now you're dead and your lessons with you.

"The stuff he left in his pack?" Our doors push the air around when they close, so you can feel it when someone comes out of his room. The whole house is connected, like some fabricated Gaia theory. I left Grant's door open a crack so I wouldn't tip off Brat.

His bag was packed and untouched. He had probably gotten it all ready before the end. It was an old sleeping bag duffel, one opening for a head with a noose around its neck. I thumbed the catch on the string and slid the mouth open. He hadn't folded his clothes, so I yanked them out at random. Under the clothes were a couple of books: ones he had read a dozen times before, but never got tired of, I guess. I could have thrown them over my shoulder, let their spines crack against the bedspread; he wouldn't have noticed the damage. I set them on the floor and told myself I'd read them some time. Dead center of the sack was a blue plastic baggie, beneath it more clothes for a pillow. I held the bag up to the sunlight and noticed for a moment that yesterday's clouds had drifted away without ever letting go their rain. I shook the bag again. It held two small, white pills. They danced and somersaulted.

"The hero loves his heroin." I opened the bag and tipped both pills out. They had been stamped, simply; Grant had probably done it himself with an Exact-O knife. One said "mem" and one said "exp". I figured the first one held the scan of Dad's brain they had done last year. If I took that, the coating would dissolve, releasing the package of bots into my bloodstream. Following bread crumbs of their programming, they'd find their way into my brain and start reconstructing based on the pattern etched into their collective memory. Everything that was me would break into the parts that weren't of themselves unique; not suddenly, with dust, as a demolition, but as though my brain was made up of colorful bricks, snapped apart one at a time and thrown onto the carpet for Mom to step on with bare feet in the middle of the night.

I thought about flushing the pill down the toilet. Instead, I put the other in my mouth. It tasted chalky, but no more so than chalk would.

"What are you doing in here?"

My back was to the door. I felt my Adam's Apple bob. I dry swallowed and almost undid myself with a cough. Guilt wouldn't be able to touch me now. I turned on my friction heels.

"Just poking through Grant's stuff to see if he had any other goodies."

His eyes were accusing; no, they weren't. They were empty for interpretation. I thought about humor and they danced with laughter. I thought about the death of his hamster and they very nearly cried.

"Got Dad's map, here." I jiggled the baggie.

"Yeah. The bath tub's overflowing."

"Shit."

I ran into the bathroom and slopped over to the tap. "You want to help me clean this up" I called, but he didn't give any answer, not even a grunt. Cursing further than I needed to, I fetched a mop and bucket. The tub was as full as it could be. When the floor was dryish, I got down on my knees to peer across the skin of water barely held inside the grip of surface tension. I wondered if I could survive drowning as easily as stabbing. But I heard that one can't drown oneself, so I'd have to get help. I wasn't ready to make that my first test, anyway. I flicked the drain release and dropped an inch or so of cold water into the pipes, closed the plug again.

"I cleaned up Grant's bag for you."

"Ah." He knew the best places to step for silence. "Thanks, Brat."

"Don't mention it, Dumb-As-A-Brick."

"You get the food sorted?"

"Yeah. And I took what's left of the olives out to the trash can."

"Bungeed the top? The dogs will love that. More so now, I imagine."

"Maybe we should give it to them."

Who would be around to lodge complaints about improper trash disposal, or, even better, for using their house as a landfill? According to Dad, we had never liked our neighbors across the street.

"Maybe we should," said Brat.

I looked at the clock. Mom and Grant would only be halfway to Spokane. We had the rest of the day free and clear, like summer is supposed to be.

"Got any plans?"

"We could play a game of cards."

"Yeah, okay."

He spread out the green felt tablecloth and sat in Mom's seat. I sat in mine. We each grabbed a deck of cards, always near to hand, and started shuffling and cutting. He was faster and smoother than I had time to practice for.

"We need one of the shuffling machines."

"What's this you two are playing then?"

"It's a trading card game. We build decks and cast spells on each other. You start the game with life, and you try to be the one with life at the end of the game."

"Who's winning?"

"We just started."

He smells like gasoline and grass clippings. Bits of thistle are lodged under his fingers; why doesn't he pull them out.

"Is there any other way of winning besides using magic?"

"Well, no. That's what the game is. Inside the context of the game, it's all the same."

"I don't know why people think they have to rely on magic."

"Damn," I say when Brandt has a good turn. Dad doesn't try to correct me, even though it was for his benefit. Now he brings his nails close to his nearsighted face and starts to pick the junk out from under them.

"I guess I'll see you boys early in the morning."

"Early?"

"We need to bring in the rest of the mulch for your Mother's garden."

"Dad."

"No complaining. I'll get you up at five-thirty."

"I have an alarm clock."

"I'll be your alarm clock."

"You lose again," says Brat, who had been paying attention to the game. He wasn't being smug, just satisfied. I could

never tell, because my Taurus blood was beating past my inner ear and I couldn't think straight. Sometimes, I stretch out my hand to help him up off the ground and halfway there I bring my stick around again into his ribs and laugh. God, I win. His eyes were ugly, joyous, empty.

"We should get some more cards," I said.

"With what?"

"I was thinking a crowbar."

"Oh. Yeah." Brat grinned. "Everybody's dead. Let the pillaging, looting, and raping begin."

"I wonder," I said as we put our cards away. "When is it that someone dies? Like, if you get eaten, do you die right away? Does your soul kinda stick in the pieces that are being digested? What if you got passed all the way through, and woke up still alive in a pile of dung, baked solid by the sun, in a desert. Dinosaurs were big enough to digest you almost whole, right?"

"You die when your brain stops."

"When does that happen?"

"When you start thinking dinosaurs and humans coexisted. I'll go find the crowbar."

He disappeared while I waited in the kitchen. All our knives were laid out on the drying towel, stained with water spots. They were alike to me. I twisted my fingers around a small paring knife. My right hand I made the snake and the left wrist wasn't anything else. I had to dig deeper into the skin than I had thought. All the movies I'd seen had shown the blood leaping out of the veins, delighted to be free despite the circumstances. Instead I had to wriggle the tip back and forth to find the vein and it wasn't easy drawing it even three inches toward my elbow, being careful not to get the tendon.

Coughing, I stuck the knife under the tap and fumbled to get the cold water on. My whole left arm was shaking drops loose and onto the floor. The definition of red.

"Shit," I muttered and gripped the left in my right to

steady them both. I stared at the wound, wanting to see the magic work. I waited; the pulses began to slow and clot.

"I found it," said Brat, leaving the door open. "Let's go." I ripped a wad of paper towels from the roll and started wiping my evidence away. I couldn't stop coughing. "Lith?"

"Yeah—" cough "—justasec—" cough.

"You okay?"

He was walking to the kitchen. I could hear his shoes scraping the carpet, then tapping the linoleum. He came around the corner and I wasn't done yet.

"Oh God. What happened?"

"Grant lied to us. He said he only brought enough for Mom."

"You took it, didn't you?"

"Yeah—" cough "—but it's not—" cough cough.

"Here." He got some water on a rag and started wiping up the floor and counter before the blood stayed behind.

"Thanks."

I watched the slow unfolding of red in the paper tourniquet. The soft fibers wicked the blood away from the wound, passing it through valleys of quilt and print. It bloomed like a fire.

"I got the crowbar." He threw the rag in the garbage pail and pulled a few pieces of cardboard across to hide it. He did it without thinking hard, as if it was an old habit or muscle memory.

"Yeah. You think I lost too much blood?"

"No, you can lose way more than that before you even get weak in the knees."

"My arm was shaking."

"From shock, I'll bet. Amateur."

I flipped him off with my left hand. He brandished the crowbar at me and flicked his eyes down to my bandage.

"You're going to want to bind that." He fished some masking tape out of Mom's desk drawer and wound it around the paper towel. "Yeah, that'll hold for a while."

"Thanks."

"Yeah. So. What was it you took?"

"Let's go get some cards."

"Probably a sex change thing."

It was muggy outside, heavy and reeking of smoke. It was Dad's pyre, blazing away, putting summer to shame. He was in the sun, and angry at us.

It was going to be a four mile walk into town to Bad Brock's Carde Shoppe. It was a couple blocks off of main street.

"Oh yeah. I think I burned down most of main street."

"No big loss. The alcohol probably went nice."

"Damn. I got the liquor store, didn't I?"

"I don't know."

"I guess we'll find out."

"Good call."

"How do you feel, Brandt?"

"Like shit."

"Oh." We walked inside a song as the rhythm section, syncopating our steps down the gravel. The song would never catch on. "Why so?"

"Because I haven't been taking my pills."

"What pills?"

"Happy pills of goodness."

"I didn't know you were on those."

"No kidding? Huh. Thought I told everybody who needed to know."

"You need to learn responsibility."

"But Dad! Grant didn't buy anything."

He had asked Mom to park the car in the yard when we got back from town so he could wash it. The cracked green garden hose lies in a coil next to his knees as he screws one of its mouths, with difficulty, into the spigot. I can see his bones hurt.

"What Grant did or didn't do is not what I'm getting at

*here, Lithium. I'm trying to raise all my boys into responsible
young men."*

*He twists the water on and aims the hose at the wind-
shield. The cascade of reclamation water looks peaceful, laying a
millimeter blanket on the plexi-glass.*

"I just bought a couple packs of cards."

*"It's not what I would have done in your case." His hands
always looked dry. I think that's why he washed the car himself. It
wasn't anything to look at, the old station wagon. But his hands
enjoyed it.*

"Do you need any help?"

*"Nope. But why don't you go ahead and send Grant on
out, will you?"*

"Yeah." His whistle follows me inside.

"Grant. Dad wants you."

*A few minutes later, Grant is up to his elbows in suds
and scrubbing down the Goodyears and I'm in his room looking
out the window.*

I kept looking at my wrist as we walked down the
grades into town.

"I wonder what it is I took."

"I told you. You're a girl, now." Brat wrinkled his
nose. "You smell that?"

"That's your first whiff of carnage, my brother."

"I somehow imagined it more like cinnamon."

"I'm not sure I ever imagined it."

"Sure you did. Everyone thinks about death. You just
weren't prophetic enough to bother about it seriously. Like
most people think about suicide. But you know how many
people say they're actually suicidal?"

"No."

"About twelve out of every thousand. You know how
many of those people say they're suicidal just to get
attention?"

"Every one I've ever seen."

"Eleven of those twelve. One person in a thousand is actually suicidal."

We walked a little further.

"Maybe there's only a thousand people left," I said, looking at him but catching only the side of his head and his sun-blushing ear.

"Maybe there's only four."

Step step. "No, there's at least five. Grant got a hold of Jema, remember?"

"Was he the one we saw at graduation, the one who hugged everybody?"

"No. That was Grant's best friend's girlfriend. Jema was the one reading out the names, I think."

"Oh. I thought she was a boy."

"Yeah."

"That's not going to help any."

"What do you mean?"

"Homosexuality terminates a generation." Step step. "I have to pee."

"Your bladder half full or half empty?" I mused, not really asking him.

"Completely full."

"I'll wait."

He scraped off the road over to a clump of sagebrush. I heard his fly go down quick and harsh, like the sound of a band-aid being pulled off. His head poked above the scrubby gray top of the bush. Then he was gone.

"Brat?"

I didn't get an answer, but the bush rustled and shook loose a few flakes of dandruff. I heard something like a dog's bark, but more wet. I jumped over the shoulder and ran to the bush.

Brandt was slumped over on his side, his left hand still around his cock. I moved it. The bush was red where his urine had hit. Bending closer, I couldn't smell anything but the normal cracked, pungent odor of the plant. Blood soaked the sparse shocks of white-ish green fronds, dripping into a darker red puddle at the base.

"Brandt." I slapped him in the face and his eyes fluttered open. "What the hell happened?"

He craned his neck toward where I was pointing then let his head fall back into the dust.

"Must've fainted."

"That's not normal."

"No, it's not. Help me up."

We gripped each other's wrists, warrior fashion. I let my fingers slide across his forearm, feeling for marks of tic-tac-toe. He did up his pants, cupping one hand around his scrotum.

"Does it hurt?"

"It aches a little."

"Has it happened before?"

"No."

"You okay to keep going?"

"Shit, Lith, it's just a little piss and blood. You already lost more than I did."

He walked bow-legged for a couple hundred yards, but gradually slid back into his normal slouch.

"I guess I know how you feel," I told him.

"That's absurd."

We came to the top of the last grade down into town. I didn't want to walk the same way as the first time, so we followed the road. I had to keep steering Brat away from the guard rail; his head was locked to the right, following trails of smoke and searching each house for movement.

"You smell barbecue?" he asked.

"Don't be funny."

"No, I'm serious. And hungry."

Mom drops the spoon. The handle clanks against the brown stained ceramic, but the head slops into the beans with a soundless splash. A cluster of brown drops hits Grandma's table. There is steam above the table and it smells so good.

"What do you mean she's not coming?"

"That was her on the phone, honey. She's having dinner with Michelle's family."

"She promised to bring the sweet potatoes."

"I know, Dorothy."

We're ready on our side. Grant hits my knee under the table and I hit Brat's and he hits mine and I hit Grant's and we all giggle. Mom glares as though she took her cranky pill and we shut up.

"Sit down, Dodo; it's time to eat." Dad's practical, he says.

"It's not holy."

"I know, dear heart. Have a seat."

Brat groaned and clutched himself again.

"What. What's wrong?"

"Just sore."

"We could rob the clinic."

"I remember you and Grant always thought you'd make great thieves, if you put your minds to it."

"We come from smart stock." Step step. "Well, half anyway."

"She got her bachelor's in psych. That's not bad."

"A five year degree."

"What's your problem?" I held up my rough band-aged arm. "We're going to have to change that, Lith. It's drying to your skin. You're kind of a selfish bastard."

"It happens," I lowered my arm and voice.

"We need to stick together."

"You're the one that runs off all the time. What do you do on the mountain?"

"I read. And indulge in being a minority."

A dog was lying on the side of the road. It was shaggy, white, and small; it reminded me of a baby. Its legs were frozen in the middle of a run and blood ran out of its mouth. Brat took a look, turned up his nose and walked in the middle of the road. My head ratcheted as we went past, following the dead fur. Its eyes were open. The gravel around its body was caught churning, like a stream coated in ripples of ice. I saw paw prints.

"Dogs are getting vicious."

"Mmm."

"Still hungry?"

"No, actually. It went away."

We stopped a block from main street at the natural foods store and each got a handful of honey sticks to suck on while we walked.

The card shop was ashes. Brat hit me on the head and we dug through the dreck for a while. We uncovered some half black boxes, but nothing undamaged.

"We could check Heath's house."

Heath used to play with us. He lived a couple blocks further from main. His family's doors were locked but the windows were big. We got bit by broken glass a hundred times. Small teeth; it wasn't anything to worry about. Heath's parents had both been doctors. We filled two garbage sacks with his collection and shouldered them.

"Ho ho ho," said Brat.

We spent the afternoon on the card table, set up next to the air conditioning vent.

"Kinda makes you feel like you figured out the cheat codes, huh?" grunted Brat. He kept returning to the metaphor long after I was tired of smiling at it.

Grant and Mom came home at six. We heard the car, and then a knock on the garage door even though it was unlocked. I stood up in a sigh and knocked back.

"We don't want any," I said as I opened the door.

Mom was asleep in his arms. She looked smaller sideways.

"What happened?" in a monotone.

"She just fell asleep."

"Whew."

"Get out of the way?"

I stepped to the side and Grant laid her on the couch, turned the wrong direction so her feet were on the throw pillows.

"What did you guys find?"

"We've got food in the trunk. What are you doing?" Brat set a glass of our water and a couple bottles of pills on the end table next to Mom's feet.

"She'll want these when she wakes up."

"She doesn't need anything. Why does super woman even need to sleep, smart feller?"

Grant gave me a look and held three fingers to his lips. "You'll wake her up. Just help me unload the car."

Red numbers that I have to lift my head for. Six-thirty. I could have slept for another half hour, if Brat hadn't gotten out his trumpet. His fingers trill clumsily. I could stay here, falling into half sleep with one foot on the floor rubbing a slow friction to and fro.

My teeth taste like battery acid. I should brush them before I eat; otherwise my tongue is going to dissolve. A quick rinse and spit. I get one of those tendrils of saliva that just dangles no matter how I smack my lips. Inhaling, it slips between my teeth, cold and slimy. I make a face so the mirror can see and spit clean.

Downstairs, Mom's hands are resting on Brat's shoulders, willing him never to stop. He does, lowering his horn to his lap.

"That was beautiful, honey," she says on her way back to the waffle iron. Her eyes are green.

Everything is. It's a good color for Christmas. Brat was the last to get out of bed and grab his stocking. Grant and I have organized our hauls into piles of candy, breakable toys, and books. Now that he's blinking and rubbing long fingers through his eyes, we can start on the big presents. Because Dad knows greed, I make sure he and Mom have their presents from me first.

"Open them."

"Oh Lithium," Mom says with her fingernail running across the top edge of the plastic ornament I had bought her. "It's beautiful. Thank you."

Her eyes are the colors of stars.

"Dad?"

Grant couldn't close the trunk because it would make a sound.

"We'll have dogs in there tomorrow."

"You've still got that wrist rocket, right?"

"Wrist rocket right," I laughed at the alliteration, which was a bad sign. "Yeah."

We had one corner of the kitchen buried under bags. "Do we have to get any of this in the freezer?"

"We weren't stupid, Lith."

"I wasn't saying you were. I was just asking."

"No, we didn't get anything that needs to be in the freezer. We just got cans and stuff."

"Love that good old fashioned stuff."

"Yeah, I'm going to bed guys," said Brat. I waved.

"I guess we can leave it here for now." Grant's eyebrows were creased, bent down because his brain was heavy.

"Listen, Grunt." I coughed into my hand, but quietly. I don't know why I did. It was a television thing. "We need to talk."

"Let's go outside, though. I need fresh air."

Wrong planet, I thought. "Okay."

It was dark and just barely more cold than warm.

"You brought other nano with you."

"Yeah. Dad's meme."

"No, there was another one."

"Have you been going through my stuff, Lith? God."

"I'm sorry. I really am. I was scared."

He felt silent. Gradually shushing out of our yard and onto the golf course, there was just enough light to see a hard line in his jaw, built strong to hold in uneducated words.

"Scared about what."

"About dying."

"There's nothing to be scared of. Not even fear. It's just a process."

"Shit. No wonder you flunked philosophy. The terror of mortality is everywhere in literature. Just knowing that every pore you're so familiar with will someday close up and stop everything: acne and growth; losing the chance to be a fuckup, of understanding God, to have the box chopped out from underneath you before the magic trick is finished. It scares me. It has every right to."

Steel, now. "You're giving flowery words to something that happens to everyone, trying to give it more argumentative weight."

"I know that. I feel heavy."

"Just pointing it out."

"I'm afraid."

"Okay." Step step. "I'm scared of losing my mind."

I nodded, and only now looking back at the black ink realize that I could have said "I told you so." We were using our fingerless words; they tumbled over and over each other, unable to manipulate what we both wanted to change. They were beautiful, quiet and dark.

"What was in the other pill?"

"Lith."

"I took it, Grant."

Without looking, he reached out a fist and boxed my ear. My skull rang, but I kept up with him.

"I know you did."

"What was in it, then?"

He sighed and bent down. We were over the fifth green, parallel to the mountain. His feet were on either side of the cup. "Ow," he muttered as he scraped a fingernail against the metal sides; I heard it, and felt a sympathetic twinge. His hand came up with someone's old ball in the palm.

"Take it." I did. "Sit down." My butt was going to get wet. "Hold it in both hands." I brought them together, lifting up the ball in offering. "Now do this." He brought his mirror hands down on the ground three times, hard. I copied.

"What now?"

"Wait a sec."

"Another experiment?"

"No this one works fine. See."

He pointed. In my hands, the golf ball was dissolving. The carbon sparkled, carried on the backs of nano like larvae on their hive's workers when the hill has been attacked by three young boys and a pint of gasoline. Frantic to complete before I know what I am seeing. The ball was gone. A piece of brown was in its place.

"What is it?"

"Bread." He took it and ate it.

"Dude. Could I do that to Brat?"

"Yes."

"You never hear about grocery accidents." I laughed through my nose. The air was too cold for my teeth.

"Very few forklifts involved. Look: we built it so it would be hard to trigger without intending to do so. How often do you touch hands and pound three times."

"It takes more than three. The average for American guys is five."

He shook his head at me and stood up, pawing at his bottom, but he couldn't get the wet off. "You don't grow up."

"Well, I don't hide it."

"You're so honest."

"I'm also the inventor of the light bulb."

He folded his hands to bar in a little warmth. "These houses don't look different, empty."

Someone's TV had been on; someone else's headlights. The Gambles' old house was spilling out gold from shaded incandescent bulbs.

"No, not really."

Hit the drain release with my heel three times; on the third, it catches and clunks. I listen to rough water elbowing through the pipes and hope it washes all of it away. Heavier with each inch. When it is down to the little dent between my hip and butt that I have when I flex, I slop to my feet. Having to pick up the papers, stained with vegetable oil and me. Dry off and make sure I'm not stuck. They belong in Grant's room.

Wrapped in my blue towel, I go there, hiding what I can next to my skinny leg, which is both of them, but only right against the wall.

He doesn't like the keyboards that don't click. They don't feel right. So he's home with both his windows open. Oh hell. I don't mind it because I haven't asked to be forgiven yet. But the paper burns. He will miss it if I put it under my closet. Wrinkles on itself. A canyon on a crevice, or the other way around, whichever reaches the shallowest.

"Dogs must have spotted a cougar," I said.

"Maybe they know the Aikres aren't around with their shotguns anymore."

"Maybe. They're smart animals."

"The dogs or the cougars?"

"Cougars."

Hand slows down because if it moves too fast I'll lose control and hit the wall with spasming and Mom will come to check on me and see the papers and the oil and she probably knows anyway. Eight times tense. Warm water is the only place to be. I lay back and hit my head on the blue ceramic, pulling my hair out of the way.

The chemicals are gone now and God takes a step forward from the shadows to whisper, Bad dumb rock you've hit the bottom again. Guilt is a mechanism to make us repent, but I can get addicted, like the Aikre kids and their guns. Stop pulling, why should I, I can't. Or ignore the impulse I'm just a boy and do what my body says. I have to twice.

The second time is with the foreskin pulled over; it's softer and slower where the first is urgent and the violence of completion is revenge.

Built by the hands of God, I am the size of a smaller ant

to him and he must have slipped. Craftsmanship sucked down the drain with my seed. I hope all of it, or Mom and Dad will find out. The second one is softer and my hands float.

I inhale. My skin divides the surface and sinks all eight inches when I want it to. Sometimes I forget that I'm holding my breath, like when I'm sleeping. I remember that exhaling is as sweet as its twin. Letting pressure off the lungs. Down then up, with out then in. A set of coordinates, Grant. In corresponds to up, out and down. Write a metaphor for an A. Find out its only B grade.

Mom doesn't want me taking baths with the lights off anymore. She's afraid I'll go to sleep and drown but I can't drown because then they'd have no choice but to find me and my eulogy won't be a time of recognizing. I open my mouth to pray and get a little water in. It tastes like salt. I spit and make a face, worse in the ripples. God built a filthy machine.

"You want the shower?" asked Grant, sighing and pushing himself up.

"Going to bed, I think. Night, Lith."

"Night, Grunt."

That night, I dreamed about an intelligent guitar that used feedback as a weapon and ran a bagel store. The robbers tried to hold us up but it made their ears bleed and mine were stopped with bits of onion. One of the robbers poked up his head as though testing the air and I could see his ears were orange, so he was okay. He shot me.

I was in a bagel shop and I saw myself being shot and then said, "Stop that, Judas!" pointing in the wrong direction then he shot me.

I saw two others being shot in my clothes and threw up, bent over when he shot me.

A tremendous howling woke me up. I went to the window and shivered. Thought hard about closing it, but kept getting distracted by drowsy thoughts of my toes in the carpet and my nakedness. The dogs were howling, and there was a lot of them. I howled back and they were silent for the space of the wag of a tail before babbling over my last echo. I closed the window, muting them but not silencing. The dark ice around me was full of shaggy colors. I closed my eyes to find the imprints that had burned in there, my life.

We sleep in the dark because, in the light, we remember too much. We can't sleep until it fades off our eyelids.

At four, Brat started playing on his computer. I smelled a toasting bagel, but I wasn't dreaming. Ladders of the lightening sky crept up my body. I couldn't get back to sleep and didn't really want to. When I could see everything clearly, my eyes drifted to the desk corner where I used to keep Gretta. I had gotten rid of her picture. The only gift of hers I had kept was a journal she gave me to write in and a nice pen. I hadn't touched either except to move them around. Equal weights settled on my chest and stomach. I got up and wrote something. I tore it up right after, but I still remember most of it. This is it:

She was a bitch when she laughed and she knew it. She used to keep a diary of stupid things I said. I loved her for that. It was green, like her contacts, which she took off when she was crying the two times I saw her cry. Once at a movie and once when she decided I wasn't good enough for her. A chess game is beautiful. A decomposing body is beautiful the same. They're both complicated. She loved to say that when I'd ask her a question. "It's complicated, Lith." Because complicated things take time, and time lets things fall apart. Everything was complicated and I never learned how to braid or unbraid her hair. She can't be missed. It's not, not my fault.

I wrote bigger. It took up almost a whole page with gold on the edge. I write smaller now because I don't know how much I will remember.

I went downstairs.

"Local lines still work," Brat said with his finger marking his place in the phonebook. He dialed, gave three rings and hung up.

"Call the airlines."

"What?"

"I heard a jet the other day."

"Miraculously, all flight attendants were spared from the molecular-level cataclysm. Praise God Almighty. How many international airports do we have in town, Lith? Two? Three?" He moved to the next name, dialed, gave three rings and hung up.

"Come have some breakfast, Lithium."

Some weight was out of place in the dining room. I had to rub the crust off my eyes before I saw.

"What's with the suitcase?"

Mom was eating cereal. "Grant thought we might be going to Los Angeles, to his lab, so I put some things together."

"Well, you don't need food or a Kevlar vest."

"I know, honey." She smiled, kinda like I do when I'm tired of Brat's repeated jokes.

Mom had set out a bowl for me. I cupped it in my hands and made the three-tap rhythm on the table top. She watched, but closed her eyes before it was completely transformed. The rim was last, sinking closer to my palms before melting like the thin frosting on an angel food cake.

I took a bite. "Can't even taste the ceramic." Another bite. "I always wanted to be a superhero. Do you remember that, Brat?"

"Yeah," he called. "You always got the energy power. I had to try and convince you that lightning wasn't energy. I did it, too."

"Where's Grunt?"

"Oh, don't bother him. He's in his room, trying to find a way to get to Jema, I think. Something about bouncing."

Brat hung up the phone. "The lines just went dead." I pointed a finger at the ceiling. Grant screamed. It was filtered through a door and distance and sounded like "fundamental mugger fashion God damn" because he opened the door and pounded down stairs. "Living in this technological hell hole!"

Mom opened up her eyelids and told him to sit, I think. He sat and glared at his useless fingers. "Your Father and I had two big arguments when we first moved down out of the mountains. One was whether we should abort Lithium. The other was about moving back to Seattle. He didn't want to. He liked it here, where the plastic was further away and you kids would have a pond and a mountain and nothing shrink wrapped. We started yelling and he went outside to chop wood. Down in the trailer park, so the walls were thin, and I could hear him, and the Parkers' dishes breaking. He was just inside the porch light, an egg of yellow light. I watched from the kitchen. He took two pieces of wood and stood them against a third. A wind started flapping the tarp over the log pile.

"Nothing he built ever fell down."

Grant ran his fingernails across the seam between table leaves, click click. One got caught. He sucked on it.

"I'm sorry, Mom."

"He made the right choice," said Mom.

"He did."

"I dunno," I said. "I would have liked Seattle, I think. Everything is more probable."

Brat was leaning on the fridge, arms folded. "Did you ever consider having me aborted?"

"No, honey."

"Why not?"

"Two wasn't the right number." She giggled. "We were going to name Grant Jennifer. You were going to be Jessica, Brandt. Your Dad suggested Zarubabel, but we thought maybe Bethany for you, Lithium."

I looked out the window.

The sun rises at five. Even if it isn't warm it fools me into wearing shorts and my sleep shirt. Breakfast won't be until six or seven, an hour before whenever Dad's shift starts. Space ships in the rosebush. Breakfast won't be until I need band-aids for my fingers. What a waste of time. Milking the sun for every last drop. Mom is in the garden. She stands up and looks everywhere around her. I think she forgot where we put the spigots. There's just lettuce right now because it grows without her hands, but we are going to have corn rows to play in. She can't see me in the corn so I can play there. The sun doesn't smell like new paint. Dirt means old. Grass means old. Rose bush thorns mean old.

"I'm going outside," I said.

"Don't go too far, honey."

"I'll just be in the yard."

"Wanna spar?" asked Brat.

"Nah."

I forgot to twist the handle when I closed the front door. The glass rattled like a snake. Turning to set it properly in the latch, I saw the scratches. Mom had repainted all the doors a year ago so they looked different when I came home for Easter. Dark green. The bottom half was torn so completely it should have been bleeding.

The door had locked behind me. I shook my head and pounded the door bell with shave and a hair cut. Brat opened it after making a face at me.

"Yeah?"

"Natives are restless, Jennifer," I said, pointing at the scratches.

"I'm Jessica. Mom, check this out."

She came over and picked at the scratches where the old paint showed light blue. "Oh darn those dogs."

"I wonder what they wanted." Brat kicked his bare toe against the smoother spaces.

"Man flesh," I said.

"Kinda makes you wonder." Grant was over, too curious.

"You sure?"

"Okay, it makes me wonder. Which species is going to evolve now? Dinosaurs got taken out, leaving room for homo sapiens. Now we're gone, so what does that leave room for?"

"A hundred thousand chimpanzees rubbing their foreheads in frustration."

I went to the edge of the porch and vaulted over the railing and low flower bushes. "Yell if you need me." The door closed once. I heard a nearby barking that had been there the whole time.

"Divex." She was a bastard. Belonged to our neighbors two doors over. Half German shepherd, half Satan's Labrador. They usually kept her chained to the apple tree. I circled around the white house with its asbestos siding from the old forties. There she was, on a chain wound down to a foot and a half, too stupid to run the other direction.

Breaking even with the edge of the garage was the trailer hitch on their SUV. A nice model. I got that close and Divex went nuts. She leapt at me and the chain pulled her down into a harsh somersault. She only squealed when her throat was too constricted to bark. Maybe she didn't like my hand on her masters' car; maybe she didn't like her masters' car, the strange beast that would take them off every day and might not bring them back. I took a step away, a step closer. She went low into a crouch and growl.

She had been running counter-clockwise. I went the same. Tall grass around her tree because she wouldn't let them mow. She snaked through it, shaking her head to get the blades out of her nose. A foot of chain, now six inches. I reached up to disconnect the chain from the tree. Warm shock lifted up my leg; I kicked. She barked and tore back her head, some of my skin coming with her. I clutched at the leash release to keep myself standing. She would die. My thumb found the catch and I let it go, falling to the other side and scrambling crab feet back, toward the Gambles' house.

"You bitch." They had had her fixed. My leg was bleeding over the bite, plugging it up. I couldn't see how bad it was. I could turn it to bread. Pain gathered around me like a cloud of gnats. Let her fix herself.

I limped home, leaving her stuck to the friction of the

metal and wood. Let her figure that out herself.

Mom freaked out when I stepped inside good leg first. She told me to get over the linoleum before I stained the carpet too bad.

"Maybe if you lay hands," I suggested to the top of her black and white head.

"What was it?"

"It was Divex. I was trying to let her off her lead."

"Oh thank God."

"Just what I was thinking. Oh God." I stumbled into the wall. I hit my head and Mom called for Grant.

"It's okay, honey. You're some right."

Grant put gauze around my leg. They stretched me on the couch. Everything started to make sense, so I spoke up. No one seemed to be listening to me.

"He's in shock," whispered Grant. ""She just missed his tendon. It's got to hurt like hell."

"We could give him some pain-blocker."

I don't know how I swallowed. Mom's hand, dry and cracked underneath the smell of lotion, the film on the pill that tasted nothing like it smelled; god damn, but the senses get confused.

After a while, I started to feel normal, again.

"Did you know William Blake had synesthesia?" asked Grant, sitting on a chair next to me.

"That's a myth." I blinked. It took a lot longer than I expected. "Why did you tell me that?"

"You just said I smelled yellow."

"Oh. I don't remember that."

"I think you had a mild seizure."

"That's a myth, too. Water, please?"

I could taste the calcium that had crusted around the lip of the faucet. It made the water warm. The only thing you can use to clean that is vinegar and vinegar is worse. The word even looks and sounds fermented, dead, stinking. The letter v and syllable gar make my lips curl because I can smell them and it's not just my nose that smells.

"What does yellow smell like, Lith? Can you find other words for it?" He shook his head and flattened a grin. "Can you describe a color to a blind man?"

"Yes." I thought. "Like wood rot – the forest wouldn't be anything without it."

Prayer is just an interruption. Grant and me were painting grasshoppers because he learned they breathe through their skin. "Come on now gather round and hold hands," says Dad. He doesn't notice that Brat is gone. I let him stay gone because he'll get in trouble that way. We say God please bless this food and thank you for blessing this day already, even though the food has been sitting out for a half hour collecting flies. God says, "Whump," and screams. If we don't say amen, that means God hears everything.

"Brandt? Brandt!" The men and women run, the grandmas and grandpas stay fretting, which means rocking back and forth. "Darn it, Brandt, say something!"

"Amen," I say, and I'm right along with them. The Brat is in the creek, but it's empty. He landed on an old bedspring. The log rotted away right under him and the bees came out upset. Ants run away and try to find a place to hide their grains of rice. Bees don't. Bees do.

Dad throws them away. I can't see any bees, just a swarm which is many bees but only one. Dad throws them away and Aftershave throws Brat's legs over his big shoulder, crawling up the leaf bank while Dad crushes them between his palms.

Eighteen stingers. Dad puts dirt on them and spits. Brat is red without words. Grant tugs on Mom's hand and says, "Mom it'll be okay, he's okay, okay" and Mom breaks a nail.

"Maybe I'm allergic to dogs," I said to Grant who was waiting for the glass. I gave it back to him.

"I don't think that's something you can be allergic to."

"I'm awfully talented. You've never managed to go to the hospital, remember. I've nearly given doctors heart attacks."

He laughed, as I was hoping he would.

"I'm feeling okay, now." I stood up into a head rush and everything went black and hot. My veins unclogged and I was back on the couch, my mouth open, stunned. "Right. Let's try that again." He grabbed my wrist like a warrior and tugged me up.

"You okay, honey?"

"Yeah, Mommy. I'm fine."

"Try putting a little weight on that ankle."

"Hey. Look at me. I'm walking."

I broke Grant's smile and went to the bathroom. I stepped on the crack between carpet and white linoleum and told her so.

"Not that it does much good, of course."

"Why don't you leave the dog handling up to me in the future, okay Lithium?" suggested Grant.

"Aye aye."

There was blood in the toilet bowl. Black on the rim, just above the water level, mixed with the dry urine and mildew that happens when you have three sons.

Brat was in his room.

"Hey. You pissed blood again."

"It's nothing." We both heard it that time. I opened my eyes to swallow his attention. "What?"

"It's a jet, you moron."

"What's so—" It struck him. "Grant!" we both yelled. He was peering out of his South window.

"It's low enough to be a drop plane," he said. "But I don't see a bucket."

"Good call. Because the first order of business is to take care of any forest fires."

"It could be military."

"Oh. Shit oh."

"What's the commotion?" asked Mom from a quiet place behind our shoulder blades. Grant and I jumped and Brat giggled a little.

"It's a bird."

"It's a plane."

"Oh God it's looking for us. See. It's sweeping."

"And mopping." Grant hit me in the breastbone with his bony elbow. I coughed and stuttered a laugh.

"Shut up! Listen!"

There was nothing different about the twin-engine whine, filtered through a thousand feet of air.

"Listen for what?"

"It's looking for us."

Mom was a couple steps further back. "No, it's probably the military. Looking for survivors."

"That's what he said. Looking for us," said Brat.

"Yeah, but he was all foreboding and stuff," I countered.

"We should go outside," said Mom from the top of the stairs.

"No! Mom, no. Wait. We can't just walk out there. We don't know what they want. They — They could have been the ones that made the virus."

"That's absurd, Grant."

"We can't know! If I knew, we'd be out of here. It's not worth it to risk. Not now. We are all we have left."

"And those nice men in the plane," I said. He hit me again and tripped downstairs for the binoculars.

Wearing pink eye shadow. Dangerous close to communist colors. I grin. That's Pedro's favorite word. Only known the guy for about thirteen hours, four playing games, and I've been a communist from his lips a hundred times already. But pink eye shadow. It sparkles back and forth to her car and her Daddy, lifting boxes to the dorm next door. She wears furry boots and jean shorts and a loose green T-shirt and pink eye shadow. I stare at her for half an hour and I don't know which room is hers. It was a rule: someone can always tell when they are being looked at. She breaks it; now it's even more a rule. I stand in my window, not naked, but praying.

A window opens. It's not her but this one looks at me just long enough to be surprised then glare. I laugh so she can see my reputation underway. Tonight will be Freshman orientation activities; playing Baby, If You Love Me until three in the morning because the best way to get to know something is to be embarrassed right beside it. I hang under sarcasm until the stars come out at eight-fifteen. We, the gangly white guys, form a cluster like a pinecone, backs all to each other like the seeds. Pedro has fun and starts braiding a girl's hair. What a thing.

The second and third floors almost all have open blinds. It must be nice to look out into the pine trees and the highway beyond, spitting streamers of light in between the trunks. She rubs off the pink eye shadow and plucks her eyebrows. From my ground-floor room, I can see from her nose up; she must be sitting at her desk.

There are boxes by the door and walls as though she were building a castle out of Kindergarten blocks. She opens one and takes the time to stretch a clean sheet on her bed. Her hands go on her hips like this and she purses her lips. I can tell because she tilts her head to do it.

Two tries, three to lower the blinds, but she figures it out and I see her silhouette.

"When were you saved?" asks Pedro even though I'm yawning every fifteen seconds and wish it was more, or less. He's on the bean bag chair with a cream soda. My room has a lock on it so I can be all by myself and I'll need to be.

"Um. I don't know. I grew up in the church. But I disagree with a few things."

"Yeah, I know what you mean," says Pedro. "I feel like I know a lot, you know? But we're going to change so much here."

"Don't know why this came to mind, but hey: we had a cat when I was growing up."

"I'm more of a dog person."

"We named her Georgia. She was an outside cat at first. Had her in the barn, mousing, and she'd rove around the golf

course and the mountain a little. She'd sit on the back porch, next to our sliding glass door, whenever we were eating meals. Just staring in. She could tell it was warm, I saw it in her paws. She was so steady, it made me feel uncomfortable. She started getting attacked by the dogs who wanted to get into her food. Beat most of them off, but she was showing it. Torn ear, a gash along her eye. We never figured out if that made her blind, if she was blind. Her paws were getting torn up. We'd had her for about two years, I think. Maybe more. She was a stray when we got her, so she must have been five or six, I'd guess. She stared inside like a gargoyle. Mom convinced my Dad to let her be an inside cat, even though Dad didn't like the idea. He opened the door and said to her, 'You have to choose, now. Inside or outside? And then you stick with your choice.' She ran right on in and spent that evening exploring everything she could fit in. Eventually, she slept in my room, on the floor next to my bed. She wasn't affectionate, but I think I was warm. A few weeks after coming inside, she started just sitting by the door again, staring outside. 'Can't let you out, Georgia.' She made a choice, after all. That was Dad's reasoning."

I pause to take a breath and try to organize my words. I never know what I'm going to say. Usually, I start into a sentence and just trust that my brain is smart enough to throw the right words in front of me.

"We went on vacation last summer for about three weeks. I accidentally shut Georgia up in my room. I didn't know she was in there. She had starved to death when we got home and I had to put an air freshener in every socket."

He yawns. So I do.

"That's a crappy bedtime story."

"That's how bedtime stories used to be."

"You're biochem, right?"

"That's what it's looking like."

We stay up telling stories as if it's a competition, and by the end we neither of us mean anything at all.

112

THREE
THE MOUNTAIN AND THE MOUNTAINS

Grant was in the storage closet under the stairs. "Tell me we have more than this one backpack."

"The external frames?" I shut the elfin door on him and opened it again.

"Yes."

"Sorry. Just that one."

"We have eight in our apartment of three."

"Well, for you suburbanites, hiking is an event. Here, it's a way of life."

He aimed a hose at me and took his thumb away from its mouth. I flinched.

"What's that doing in there?"

"I don't know." He spoke it as one syllable. He tossed the hose out to uncoil on the carpet. Mom was opening and closing cupboards. I wandered into the kitchen.

"Why bother." Brat was there too.

"You don't need to take food, Mom."

"We could be gone for quite a while."

"Yeah, I know. Brat. Come here a second. I want to demonstrate."

"You and your super powers," said Brat. "I'm the only normal human being here."

"What about Grant?" I asked.

"Super-intelligence." Brat tapped his forehead.

"Should I get water, then?" asked Mom.

"Humanity is screwed." I grinned.

"Should I get water?"

"Yes, Mom," called Grant. The jet was still thrumming the panes of our windows, growing and fading like a biorhythm. I went to watch for its vapor and silver body. Why didn't they land? Because they could see us just fine from up there; our hot bodies and sounds of boring life setting off klaxons and piercing a middle finger straight through to heaven, where God holds his beard with one hand and his eyes with another, shaking his head. His long hair swishes the clouds and air; the jet compensates and keeps its nose straight.

"Tell me why we're running," I said.

"Because I have a good imagination," said Grant, hollow from inside the closet.

"I don't have an imagination," put in Brat. "I say we stay here and just wait. Even if it's the army, they could be trying to find survivors."

"Yes," said Grant, laying open the backpack on the kitchen table. Double-handfuls of dirt spilled onto the floor.

"To help, I meant."

It was a plastic frame, so it didn't make as much noise as Grant would have liked when he threw it down. It bent and crunched on the linoleum and he threw up his hands.

"We have to do something! I am the oldest, so I am going to lead. We will be alright."

"I am older than you, Grant, honey."

"Eldest," I said.

"No you're not, Mom. This version of you, it's only

as old as since I gave you the nano." I saw a smirk start to form at the corner of Mom's mouth, but she killed it quickly in the face of Grant's double-eyed earnestness. "Start filling bottles with water. We'll need them. You two. Go get a few warm clothes and your thinnest blankets." We didn't. "God! Go!" We didn't look at each other but we went.

"Grant. Are you sure?"

"If I was sure about anything, Mom, you'd all be unconscious and I'd *drag* you the whole fucking way."

"Where are we going?"

"Into the mountains."

He hands me our water bottle, even though it's his. He keeps it around his waist and it tastes a little like metal. Mom said don't use Kool-aid, but we used the green kind. We can see down into town. I can't make out the school because the mill makes a haze of steam over everything, like my eyes. I keep blinking to change it.

"Look over there."

Grant twists me on my heels. We are at the top of my tallest mountain and it isn't so tall anymore. It has brothers. Straight across is only halfway up the next older mountain. Grant says, "There's a family that lives over there whose Daddy got rolled under a tractor," but it's a silly story because no one can live over there. Over there doesn't exist like right here exists, under my feet, and it doesn't matter if God created the universe only yesterday because I can remember it under my feet and I have it under my feet and it's time to take my shoes off and fill the sink with the dirt from my feet. So we race down the backside, the closest I can get to not existing, and we make up stories about how we went so fast that time went backwards and we saw a rattlesnake unbite a girl's leg, but we didn't look at her leg.

While Grant was licking at responsibility, I drove into town again. He caught my little bundle of clothes in his left hand and raised an eyebrow at me. "I'll be right back."

"Where are you going?"

I closed the door, knowing that his control was only in his words. Only. I was kidding myself but I turned it into a harsh ratchet on the ignition key and a chunk of blue smoke. I drove slow enough to turn my head to both sides, pulling in all the rectangles and the dogs and the triangles and the cats and the trees. My eyes were a vortex. I don't have any memories without pictures. Nothing of pure sound, or pure taste. I can see it all. This is what haunts the soldiers when the war is over. The harrowing explosions are etched onto the eyes, as they used to think the killer's face would be.

I have my town in my eyes, laid over all its other iterations. I can dig them all out, but it feels as though I am clawing straight along my optic nerve. I stopped chewing on my fingernails a week ago.

I pulled the town in. Blinked to keep the smoke soft over my eyes. A rumble through the ground, not the air. Across the bridge, on the other side of town, something was moving. Another motor. I got out of the car and snuck closer. I hid around the pizza shack and dipped my head out. A painted flag and halftrack treads. A mammoth seventy-millimeter finger stabbed out at me, half a mile away. It crawled into my eyes. The pupils are holes.

I ran back to the car and didn't care when it choked on the way up the grades except if it would leave me as a tired, unwatered mule would. Stomped with one foot, kicked with the other, and felt a finger in the small of my back and dead television stares.

"Where have you been?"

"Leave me alone. They're on the ground."

"The military?"

"Yes."

Grant was fighting through some invisible spider webs, his arms picking pieces out of his way and his lips moving. "We'll take turns. If only we had another backpack. I estimate we have about a week's worth of water on this."

"Why are we running?"

"I don't know, damn it!" As if I were the one that

spun the webs. His fingers barely missed me. "Get Brandt. And where's Mom?" He was slinging the pack across his shoulders and clicking the straps. "We need to go. Now, we need to go."

"I'll get them."

Brat was playing on his computer.

"We're leaving, Brat." He saved his game and quit, standing with his hands resting quiet outside his pockets. He followed me into Mom's room where she was hunched against her closet, one hand on its golden leaf handle.

"Mom. It's time to go."

"I can't, honey."

"Mom." Brandt got down next to her and put his hand on her elbow, the part she couldn't kiss. "Grant says we need to go."

"With his hands, Brandt honey."

"We don't have time for this," I said without passion, figuring that Grant's impatient drumming feet would add enough in the soundtrack.

"With his two hands and broken finger nails."

Brat crossed his legs and rocked back. His arm had to stretch further to keep her and it looked uncomfortable, like praying, clasping hands when you have an itch right between your eyes and can't even stare at it to make it go away.

"I can't leave this house. My beautiful children. I'll be alright."

"You can't survive a mortar shell, Mom." I was sneering so she smiled at me. "You'd be turned into vapor." She gripped the closet until her knuckles were edged in red.

"Too small to do anything with," said Mom.

Dad knocks on my door. He always only knocks twice, if he thinks I might be asleep. Mom knocks three times. Once to stop the dreams, once to open my eyes, once to get me out of bed. I'm not asleep and not dressed. I pull on my wadded boxers with today on them and open the door.

"Yeah?"

117

He tosses the pile of dirty papers in my face. I close my eyes in time. I hear them fluttering and bending to touch themselves. I don't want to open my eyes.

"*You left those in our bathroom.*"

"*I— Did Mom see them?*"

"*Look at me, son.*" *I open my eyes.* "*No, she didn't see them.*" *What had I done? Oh, I remember with a strange pulse of cold that's too late, as though remembering a bad grade I got from Mister Jakobs. I put them under the bathmat so they wouldn't get too wet so Grant wouldn't notice.*

"*This kind of thing. It isn't very respectful to the ladies. Or the men.*"

"*Sir. I didn't mean disrespect. I don't even know them.*"

"*If you did.*"

What do I say to put you to bed? It's only one thing. It's only an uncomfortable need to drain the pressure before I damage my insides. It doesn't get complicated until after, in the water, in my own filth.

He turns out of my blue computer light and starts down the hall to his own room.

"*They're Grant's.*"

He stops. Opens his door and shuts it dark behind him. Tonight's last breeze sneaks in through the slid window because my door is open and it won't have to stay long. They crinkle and fold to touch themselves.

"She doesn't want to come."

Grant didn't even answer. He just went upstairs. I got a glass of water and listened to his footsteps through the kitchen ceiling go to Mom, then away. The bathroom door rattled open. I didn't hear the toilet flush. The counter was clean. I hopped up on it, banging my head against a cupboard and cursing. It echoed. I heard, "No!" and mumbles, then heavy footfalls. Brat and Grant carried her down the stairs. She was limp.

"What?"

"We gave her a dose of her relaxant."

"We," said Brat with a chuckle.

"She didn't want to come, but we can't leave her." I screwed up my eyebrows at Brat and he just shrugged at me with his shoulder and her feet.

"How long will she be out for?"

"Well, we're leaving now. Where are you going?"

"Just a sec."

I went to my room and pulled it in. Four friends had each given me bookstore leather-bound journals as graduation presents, plus the one I had from Gretta. I didn't need that many. I stuck two of them balanced in my cargo pockets and snatched Gretta's pen from my desk, clipping it onto my waistband.

Brat set Mom's feet down. She shook the house; the china rattled in the hutch she had inherited from Grandma before the testament was read.

"You get her, Lith. I'll get the door."

Grant, still cradling Mom's head, gestured with it. "Then you get the pack first, Brandt."

"Fine." He slid open the glass door and I could smell the mountain rotting in the summer heat. Its own heat, summoned by the sun, atoms shaking. We could feel it. Nothing is too small to feel.

"You get her head," said Grant, moving around.

"We can't move fast enough, Grant," I said. "They had tanks, or something."

"They can't care about us that much." Brat's back was to us.

"Out of the way. And they can. They do. I don't want to know why. I would rather be forgotten."

"We can't move fast enough."

"Yes, we can, Lith. Just keep your brain up. That's what wins a game of chess."

"I played computer games."

"Take her head."

"Got it."

We scraped down the steps. We were both taller than her, but she must have weighed a hundred eighty, at least. I played computer games and chopped wood.

Brat stomped down the knapweed so we wouldn't get much in our socks. She opened her eyes straight into mine and burnt a few words of nonsense into my bare ears.

"Smarmy action figure. Set me up right up another."

"Yes, Mom—" She interrupted with more. Her tongue would burn. It was crackling. That and the dry weeds underneath my shoes, snapping as though they were bones, except bones wouldn't break so easily. I could grind them up to make my bread.

We fight in front of the golfers to give them something to do. Spinning is stupid; they just do it in the movies because you look cool when you wear a cloak. Fighting with a cloak on is stupid. How many broken thumbs do the actors get? One and a rush to the hospital. Mom didn't know about the last one until I couldn't pick up a glass of milk. Brat is on his back but he still has both his arms so I need to be careful.

He scythes across the short grass. I leap and bring my sword across my chest in a slash. When he is there I am here. His left shoulder grunts and hisses. With his right, he switches the direction of his sweep and catches my ankle when I land. Right on the ball where I fall over, laughing like heh heh heh heh from the bottom of my throat. Brat stabs. On my side, I take the skin across his wrist with my edge. He falters and I drop his head. He spread eagles.

"Your game." If I stop now, he will get up and get me. He grabs my sword with both his hands and wrenches it out of my fingers. "I said your game." I have splinters in my fingers and he on his wrist.

An old man shakes his head and misses his putt.

I stand up, rolling a little off my ankle. I pick up my sword. Brat is still on the ground. At his feet, I hold out one end for him to grab. He does, with one hand. I wrench it out of him,

120

through his palm.

"That's for the splinters. Eye for an eye."

"Count again." He pokes at his palm, picking with chewed fingernails at the tiny slivers standing straight or flat, out of his skin or into it.

I was first, walking half backwards, my hands under Mom's armpits. I had to keep resetting my grip. Brat was along next to us. He would bounce his step every ten or so and smile at me. She was asleep again, completely. We were across the golf course and working on the first bit of uphill.

"Why don't you go ahead, Grant."

"No. Her head is heavier. It needs to go first."

"Yeah," I agreed.

None of us had a watch, but I guessed two hours before Grant set down her feet and said,

"We should take a break."

"We're not making good enough time." I was gazing at the summit, drifting my eyes down across the rubble from ancient rock slides. I stamped my feet on the granite boulder under me. "Brat gets a turn, now," I said, setting Mom's head on a clump of moss.

"Yeah. Give the pack to Lith. Get some water out, Lith," he added after I had slung it over my back. I elbowed back out of it and slid open the zipper. Brat was blinking out across the golf course, but I didn't know what wall his eyes came up against, how far they went. I tried to tell by the reflection in his pupils, but he got self-conscious and turned them at me and then there was nothing to see.

We shared some water. Grant tried to get Mom to open up and take a few swallows. I heard her spit it up.

Dust was swirling up from the town. Or smoke. "We need to go faster."

"Think we'll get press-ganged if they catch us?"

"Grant and me, maybe. You're too scrawny."

Brat laughed. "Let's hear it for the skinny white guy."

I looked down at a scratching sound. Mom's fingers

were spidering through the dust and gravel, clogging up her nails. Not frantic. They reminded me of that blind man's eyes in the documentary they show in twelfth-grade health. The one about medical nano. Right before the segment about the cure for impotence. He can see for the first time. His eyes don't care that he'll never be able to sleep again; they burn every angle and sunspot into his retina, afraid that some day it will all go dark again. Her hands felt every grain of dirt.

A dog howled. With the echo off the mountain, each of us whirled a different direction. After a beat, I laughed with my lips.

"Come on," said Grant. "We need to keep moving."

The last quarter of the hike always takes the longest. By that time, it was Brat and me, with Brat on her head. We almost dropped her when Brat slid backwards on loose rocks and bent his elbow the wrong way. Grant had to carry her after that. She would have tumbled onto one of the slides. By the time we made it to the top, she was shaking and the sun had nearly set. The stupor was wearing off. She was getting clearer and dimmer.

"Did anyone bring a flashlight?"

"The flash?"

"That's a flask."

"A fish?"

"The flutes."

"That's a resounding no, big brother."

"Get down, will you two? Backlit like this, we must stand out like a set of beacons on a hill."

We scrambled over the lip of the mountain. Brat got one of the bottles of water and took a drink. He popped something into his mouth and washed it down. Grant was making a bed twenty feet from the black shadow of Dad's pyre, down the other side.

"What did you just take, Brat?"

"Nothing. My medication."

"Isn't that in the mornings?" asked Grant.

"I forgot this morning."

When the sun went all the way down, I turned back to the summit. The city is always bigger at night. During the day, you just see the trees; the buildings almost don't exist. At night, there are street lights and porch lights, television screens and the airport floods. The trees hide it all, but it sneaks out when you can't see the trees. Lights were made by hands, like stars. I looked up into the blackening sky and could see them. They hated me, so big that they papered the sky. Not like the trees that go invisible and leave.

"Bye, Lith." He had come up behind me like a ghost.

"G'night, Brat. You want anything to eat?"

"Not out of your hands. I know where they've been."

I slipped behind him, out of the town's view, and sat down next to Grant. There was no fire. Brat curled up next to Mom and put a hand on her elbow, tendering his own.

"You want anything to eat, Grunt?"

"Yeah."

I reached for a couple stones and fit them into my palms. They were greasy. I wiped my thumbs across their noses. A thin layer of black. I held the stain out to Grant.

"Say good night to Dad." He turned his face away.

"Come on, Lith."

Three mortar-and-pestle slams on the dirty ground. It was full dark, now; the only light was that which bled around the top of the mountain and made the scraggly trees majestic. I tested my hands. The bread was done in one loaf. I broke it in half and passed my left hand over to Grant, but overshot in the dark. He reached out to grab it and thumped my chest.

His fingers paused then flattened over my heart. I heard him lean forward. I didn't move. He smelled like soot and a new book.

The bread was cold. He sat back and ate his half.

"Fmf gmf."

"Swallow," I said.

"Not bad."

"Thanks. I made it myself." I took a small bite. "Can it taste any different?"

"No. It's just carbon."

"So? We are too, but we don't taste the same."

He took another bite and must have let it dissolve in his mouth, because I didn't hear his jaws working.

"You're thinking like an English major. When words are the end of it."

"Words are ideas."

"No. Words can't be ideas. Ideas don't come out."

"Really. What about this idea. God says, I am disgusted with the world and its parts, walking around separate like they didn't even know it's all a whole; and when you cross this street, you're crossing her, and when you sleep with this girl, you're making me angry; and when you step on a crack, you send a rocket to the moon; and you don't know it and you don't deserve it. I will turn you over and start you over."

He stretched out his legs and reminded me of my own. I uncrossed them and felt the blood lines across the undersides of my thighs complaining with the hot red through them again.

"Is that how you think it went?"

"I dunno. I was pulling that out of my butt."

"You know what I think?"

"That's not what I think."

"I know, but do you know what I think?"

"Something about twins."

"Yeah. In a way. We were too damn homogenized. You could take a hundred of us, stick us in a bottle, do a little dance with it, pour us out again, and I wouldn't notice if I had someone else's arm, leg. Brain. Not me, I mean. But almost everyone I met. They used to call America a melting pot. That's the most goddamn stupid intention I ever heard. And we liked it. We begged to be destroyed and stirred up and poured into identical molds. Movies all the same. Breast size all the same. Eye color, intonation, wardrobe. It felt good to be the same. And that's what did it. Everyone had the designer nano in them, dormant or not. That's where they attacked. Right at the root."

"So anybody who didn't have the nano would have survived?"

"That's statistically impossible. Everyone in North America at least would have breathed in millions during the last three years."

With a stick, I drew invisibly. "You really think it was the military?"

"I don't know."

The word is Revelation. Not plural: singular. As if it were the most important one, the only one that mattered. God didn't need to speak anymore. Got it covered, Abba. Signed, your obedient servant, John. Then I dreamed. I dreamed rainbow jewels and terrifying holiness that lost its terror but none of its fearsome pride when I realized that it was coming from my own throat in the quiet assurance that no one would be poorer if I ever ceased to sing. Then I dreamed. I dreamed that I was in the burn unit and watching corpses roll past on squeaky gurneys and I knew I was in a dream and that made it so much worse because in a dream you can't go back to sleep you're always awake and have to keep your eyes open and have to see theirs burned shut and the red and black especially the black which makes up everything all burned down into flaking pieces that once they break off hold nothing of the soul and their teeth stared at me and they didn't have nipples or breasts and they stared at me and I couldn't go to sleep and I couldn't go back to sleep.

Then I stopped dreaming. A plague sweeps across the nations while God's away tending to another planet and keeping Jesus from making a big mistake this time. Limbs atrophy and drop off; the stumps get infected. We call it the green plague and everything about it makes you sick. The hungry eyes of children who don't care if you give them rice or roll over and die so they can eat your flesh. Humanity curls up like pill bugs or the loser. And then they're gone. Decomposing, fertilizing the next wave of intelligence. This didn't happen. I'm so much like God.

"We'll never know, will we?"

"I don't think so. I don't know where we're going. And when we get there, I don't know what good it's going to do. We could stay up here in the mountains for a while, and then try to go back to town. We're going out there." I saw his outline nod out into the other mountains.

"I'm tired," I said. It wasn't cold. I heard him turn off his mouth and then his words were only spoken inside his thick head. That was good enough. He rolled onto the ground. Stars came out when his silhouette slid away. Mom and Brat were both shaking so I went to them. Mom would shake, contagious as a yawn, then Brat would shake. I felt myself shiver on the shoulder blades but it wasn't that cold.

The dogs were howling that night. I didn't sleep or comfort the other three. My back was against a rock. The dogs howled, together, as if without their owners they could now become their true selves, the way a child will act when his parents are out of town for the weekend. Throw a party, invite all the girls you *know* watch you through a telescope, hunt down a cat and eat it raw without fear of the air rifle or the boot. I could hear joy in the echoes.

The waxing moon hovered on a string above our camp. All three of their heads were pointing toward me. The hair on my brothers' heads was short, Mom's was going silver and more. I picked a lock of my own off my forehead and fidgeted it into knots. The free radical. Mom and Dad had gravity and held the other two in close orbits. If I got up, took my share of water and left the pack, it would be the end. It wouldn't matter. I kicked a rock down the slope. Its bone on bone clacking didn't even make Mom shudder near to wakefulness. They needed me; they didn't. I looked down at my hands, unfolding each finger and chewing off the fingernails that glinted sullen in the moon's light.

I opened up the journal and bit the cap off the pen. For a while, I wrote what I could remember without having to see the words. That made it okay. Dawn came; the ink went uninvisible more deliberately than I did.

"Wake up." I kicked Brat enough to make him bite his tongue.

"Lithium."

"We should be moving. It'll keep you warm." The sun was shining and already hot enough for me to roll up my sleeves. Brat rose, one muscle at a time as though he had forgotten how they worked.

"There were rocks under my back."

"No kidding?" Then he brought his fist down in the dirt, winced, and picked a sharp piece of gravel out of the heel of his palm.

"Right," he whispered.

I kicked Grant and prodded Mom in the shoulder.

"I was already awake," grumbled Grant.

"Sure."

"I had my eyes open."

"My mistake. If it happens again, you can feed me to the dogs." I waved a hand but nobody howled. It was enough to chill my spine.

"Can you hear anything, Brandt?" asked Mom. Brat was standing, head cocked in the direction of the town.

"No. Nothing."

"Who wants breakfast?" I had made a few flat loaves when the sun was starting to rise on the rest of the wilderness. Its rays shot over our heads, built up against the front of the mountain, bled their heat through rocks and air.

They reached out and slow.

"What super power do you want I call energy which means lightning too, okay?" Grant is wearing a sheet the wrong way round. I wanted to play Lion Tamer.

"You always call energy."

"Mud," says the Brat on his knees which are his feet.

"That's not a power, Brandt.""

"Lotsa mud."

"Okay okay I got it," I say. "I want to be able to stop time."

127

"Yeah, but you use that once and then you'd never be able to use it again, cuz you'd stop yourself, and then you'd never wake up again."

"So I stop time for other people. Everyone but me."

"Mud mud mud."

"But then you couldn't breathe or move because without time, the air doesn't move. Time is everything." He checked out a book from the library last week and Mom just told me to wait until I could read as if they weren't all full of pictures anyway. Pictures bigger than my head.

"So I'll stop time except for around my bubble."

This is the powers game and we never actually get to test them out. The game is arguing about our powers instead of showing the world and ants and golfers what we can do.

When we go back inside, Dad stops us and checks our feet. The Brat has mud up to his knees so Dad sprays him with the hose and he runs off crying to Mom.

The sound of a rattlesnake always makes me look at my feet. I stepped on one, once, because I didn't. God didn't know he had made blue jeans, but I told him so then and thanked him, too.

Mom was in the front, now, and she heard it at the same time as the rest of us. It was hard to tell where it was coming from.

"Don't move, children," she said and took another step forward. After it moved, we could see where it was. Toasting itself on a rock that hadn't been warm for more than half an hour, as slow as the sun was rising. It flashed out at Mom in bright brown and sunk its fangs into her shin. She was just wearing a pair of girl jeans that don't stop anything, especially lust; or, I guess, especially rattlesnake venom. She winced and brought her other heel down on its head.

"You okay?" one of us asked.

She shook her leg like a dog's, stamped the foot a couple of times, and grinned.

"Yep. I'm just fine. Let's keep going."

Brat was in the rear and kept falling behind. I would turn and look at him and he would take years to meet me. The rims of his eyes were confused and went to me for help but I can't imagine mine were any more rigid and assured. I clapped him on the back, once, and said, "We'll be alright."

"I told you so," he replied and sped up to walk with Mom.

It wasn't long before Grant and I started arguing. Our feet were on different soil, now, and socks were filling slowly with grass seeds. We disagreed about what this mountain was called. A map I once saw said it was called Grass Seed Mountain, which I had thought was odd and that's why I remembered it. Grant insisted that it was something else named after Mister Gamble, or Mister Juarez, or someone old we once knew.

Brat rounded on us.

"I told you three! I don't want to hear this back and forth. If you can't convince the other guy in two tries, just be the bigger man and give it up!"

He went back to Mom's side and held her hand. I could see the squeeze.

"It worked for the Catholics," I muttered and almost felt the hose.

"They had thumbscrews," said Grant; a big sacrifice. He left me in a cloud of dust as he hurried to catch up with Mom and Brat. He slowed and laid out a brotherly hand.

"Why did you take it, Brandt?" I could hear. He wasn't trying to be quiet or calm. "I thought it was Lithium." I was stumbling forward, trying to get there quietly enough to hear the words before the words got too scared.

"No. It was me."

"Why."

"Don't question me."

"I know that's you, Brandt."

Brandt, who started to quiver and couldn't find his next foot to put down.

"Brandt, honey? What's—"

"It's not safe. It could kill you."

"Me too," he said, each letter chopped off between his chattering teeth.

"We never tested a map on a breathing man."

"Don't you understand! I'm ready to die! I've been ready to die since I was eight years old!"

"Why are you still alive?" I wondered, and I hope it was only in my head. When the mind goes, does God realize it? Will Brandt be dead when Dad takes over completely, or will Dad have to fight for every synapse and neuron. If Dad wins, my brother will be gone and I could touch him.

I put out both my arms from behind him and swallowed him in a bear hug as fierce as his times alone on the mountain. Mom was bent down in front of him. She looked into his eyes. He shook but didn't try to throw off my hands.

"I know when your sight stops at your eyelids, honey. Look at me." He didn't move but he did and Grant was on the ground now with a rock in his hand. He ground the rock in his hand.

Brat passed out, going limp in my arms. I almost dropped him. Mom helped me make him look comfortable.

"We're stopping here tonight," she said.

"Mom. No. We're still facing the town." There it was. We had climbed high enough that I would be able to see the lights when the sky gave up.

"We can't move with him like this. Grant. Can I talk to you?" Her head was looking straight up because she knew how cliché it was to stare at her toes and his body. They went off together, just far enough away from my ears to make me not care. I was the one with the pack, then, so I took out the one thin blanket we had brought and stretched it over my brother. He shook and hit his head on a rock. I moved it out of the way. His teeth were grinding. I found a stick and jammed it between them, catching one finger between his incisors.

We still had hours before the sun fell over behind the

mountains.

Mom and Grant came back and both their faces were scraped free of tears.

"Lithium—"

"I'll go make us some lunch, shall I?"

"Don't get angry at me."

"Fuck you, Mom. You couldn't get more for yourself." I didn't mean it. There's no way I could have meant it, and she knew it, but Grant choked and her eyelids drooped and Dad shuddered on the ground and spit out the stick.

I have had enough of nearly failing classes because she changes her mind and wants to talk to me and only finds a few words like "I'm not angry at you," "Wait, please wait," "I never needed you," "I guess it hurts when you look at other girls." It's exhausting and I shouldn't wake up every morning straight into the face that vomits me around. School policy says we're not allowed to have fires in our rooms. No birthday candles or lighters. Incense is okay as long as no one complains and I complain. So I take the pile to the bathroom, to the one tub. It has a curtain around it; the only shower on the floor with a curtain. So it's called the Masturbator.

The taps squeak when I start it filling. Both pipes wide open, though the nose can only shoot so much out at any time. My palm goes flat and back and forth, making holes in the water's skin. Water heals. Prometheus had to steal fire because it was power the gods didn't want us to have; but water we have had since the beginning of time. Water was the power that the gods didn't know about. Our roots can't grow inches without it. Inches and feet. Because I'm out of that sterile building where I have to wear shoes and we measure everything in centimeters and meters. Six inches in the tub, now. Water is the power for the whole state and it's where we came from. It's the fires of Mount Doom, the furnace that the sword was forged in, the hand that shaped the clay. The only place where these can be destroyed.

The hot water must have run out. It's only gushing cold,

131

now, and that's okay because voodoo isn't real anymore. I drop the pictures in and push them down beneath the skin. The ones that are face up I turn around so they will drown. I close the curtain and go back to my room, putting staples in the walls in letters and designs. Chunk chunk, they bend in on themselves chunk click empty.

"Apologize to your Mother."

I ran away, further up. It would be okay if I didn't turn around. Behind a tree, I stopped and listened. Nothing in the air, no words or satellites. I bent my head into the two points of my thumbs and cried and wrote, both the same.

When I got back to the camp with four loaves, Brandt was sitting up with the blanket wrapped around him like a poncho.

"How," I said. I held out my arms and he took all four loaves.

"Make some more, Lith," said Grant. "He needs his strength. I guess."

Mom had one hand over her womb and the other over Dad's knee. I saw them both moving like spiders, never going anywhere. Massaging life from her own skin to his.

It was starting to get dark. Grant tossed me a bottle of water.

"A lot of rock slides up ahead," I told him. He knew, I knew. If you had asked either of us to describe the mountains to a painter, you would have gotten a piece of pastel art for a doctor's waiting room; nothing to distinguish the scene from any other in America. But you show us a picture, and we can could tell you that this rock was the first one we saw whenever we crested the ridge and this one looked like a penis when I turned thirteen. We knew the place like the tops of our feet.

"Yeah. That's why Dad needs his strength. We won't be able to carry him."

A great cacophony of howls blew like wind through our hair and played with the blankets.

132

"Does it sound like they're getting closer?" Grant wondered, standing up.

"It sounds like they're all that's left. So they're everywhere."

"Not your poetics, Lith."

"Hey, Mom," I said, turning to her. "What's the deal with wanting to have me aborted?"

She took it head on and let it split around her. She gave me a sad smile and waited for an apology. Let her keep waiting. She's never done the courtesy and water and I already have an understanding.

"You die when your brain stops."

I went off by myself again. No one protested. There was shade, nestled in a rocky outcropping, that would last all night. I brushed away a few pine needles, but not all of them. Something was muttering off my rubber lips before I could even sit. I opened my mouth and cracked the skin off my vocal cords. To sing, which I'm not very good at.

I sang to purify the under parts, the ones that couldn't see because they were inside of me. We begged to be laid open, skin and all unhealed. To see. To feel the kind of rain that actually sloughs the blood, the poison from the mechanics of the pieces, of the puzzle, of the unbearable organization with every part unwasted. Perfection rubbed my hand across the sharp edge of a rock over and over to friction numb the nerves laced through the skin like street lights and stars. I went too far and cut the palm open, right at the roots of my fingers. It didn't hurt until I looked and then it hurt like water.

"Ah. Green's your favorite color." Pedro's bed and sheets and pillowcase and computer monitor. He lifts a corner of a blanket and lets it fan down.

"Someone else picked all that out. Well," he amends with a driven grin. *"Except for that."* He taps the air at his computer.

"That was to piss off my Dad."

"He doesn't like green?"

"He works in an office building."

We talk more and deeper, latching onto music and books, wishing that we both were dharma bums. Like plugs fitting into place, we live a happy moment. His roommate's bed is a mess of ugly quilt and Canadian plaid. I lay on it without my smell. He finally tells me her name is Heather and she gave the green to him as a going-away-good-bye-forever present. I finally tell him that college doesn't know it, but here we are, finding a friend like finding a job. I lay on his roommate's bed and take the moment to home.

But Pedro was dead and he didn't know it. They all were dead and couldn't have known it except for a few seconds of melting terror that left them at the same time as their souls, going in an opposite direction. Direction doesn't matter. Just away from here.

A dog called and was answered. A chain of grated syllables leapt from throat to throat but I had stopped singing.

"Lithium. Out here by yourself. It's not safe."

"Brat."

"No, son. I won't be."

He sat down next to me, a stranger. If I glared, he wouldn't care, so I started folding a pine needle into my name.

"Heard what you asked your Mama." His voice was still squeaking, like Brat's. He wasn't making an effort to weigh it down with the sort of chest rumbling baritone that sometimes helped my brother out in front of the girls. I wished he would.

"What's that."

"Seems like a strange thing to ask about. Why would you wanna think about that?"

"You could tell me."

"Yeah. Yeah, I could." Compassion was trying to

134

fight its way out his fingers but got stuck on the dead fabric of his nails. "Still a strange thing."

"She brought it up. After you died."

"Ah. That. Can't really say I died though can we?" He chuckled.

"You did." I said, "You creepy zombie bastard," and didn't feel the chiding knuckles I expected. He wouldn't hit me. He would rap me where my shoulder met my neck, asking me if I would please let him in. He didn't even do that. He leaned back on his arms. His elbows popped. He made a face. His elbows wouldn't pop. He never popped them. Not like Brandt. Brandt popped every bone he could reach.

"I've got a better story I'd like to tell you, though. Dodo and I didn't have very many as you'd call dates. Not real ones. We were home bodies, and didn't go out much. Twice when we were courting. One of those was when I proposed. Third time I took her out into the forest right before a clear cut. The fourth was on the day you were delivered. We figured we had three weeks until you were due, and she was getting so stressed trying to keep our budget up and little Grant satisfied. We found a cheap baby sitter. Grant liked the blondes, you know. I took her out to a nice restaurant and held her hand the whole time. When she squeezed it, I thought she was just being affectionate, but when I looked at her eyes she was scared. Lith, she was scared. We rushed over to the hospital and you came out trying to turn sideways. God's grace and the doctor's hands kept you from tearing a hole right through her. She passed out and they had to take you to one of their machines, to breathe for you or something like that. When they decided you weren't going to die on us, they asked for a name for the certificate. Dodo was still asleep, so I had to answer. I swear I heard them right, and I swear I tried to say, 'Justin', but my brain heard 'Is she on any medication?' and all I heard out my own mouth was 'Lithium', so that's what they put on the certificate. That's what made it all legal." He laughed, then, and kept it in the smile. "We never had to pay the check at

135

the restaurant. Funny time."

"A scream."

"Well, there was that, too."

Then he vomited all over me and passed out. I didn't look up that whole time, but that made me. I carried him over my shoulder because I was still taller and I was still stronger. Mom took him into her lap and didn't care that her breasts were dangling over him. Grant poked at the ground with a stick and I tried to clean the bile off my hands. The smell sat in the valleys of my fingerprints and wouldn't budge.

"We should build a fire," said Grant.

"What about the dogs?" I asked.

"Forget the dogs."

It's getting a little harder to write. I think my pen is running out of ink. Grant used to make me lick our coloring pens to get them going again, but those were felt. This black ink doesn't taste very good. Maybe if I turned my tongue to bread. Or didn't waste my

The next morning, I woke up with an uncomfortable hard-on. I was the first up. I couldn't do it around here; I had to go somewhere else. Out of camp, back to the rock. I beat myself raw. It would have gone faster if I had closed my eyes, but I left them open and hungry. The one mass of pink flesh captured in my memories kept rolling over and over. I ignored it and loved the sun coming up. As I imagined warmth hitting the top of my head, warmth rushed out of me and over the edge. I cleaned myself up as best and painfully as I could with a handful of pine needles and moss. The smell would bring the dogs.

Not wanting to go back to camp and make breakfast just yet, I wedged my toes into the slippery dirt and played chicken with the line of morning as it came down the mountainside. Stopped full in the light and didn't know anything.

The sun goes down and the service begins. Brat reads the scripture. Mom and I are in the choir. So is he. He runs across the front of the church to be with us. Deep bass and I'm a breathy

tenor. Mildred lifts up her arms and we fake discipline and from the diaphragm. Dad's voice and mine battle for the melody, clawing our notes to the top, but in the end it's Mom that clenches it between her teeth with the other sopranos. Jesus would have died for harmony. The song pumps my blood and ends so Dad can go back to read the scripture.

I think Good Friday is so much more powerful than Easter. Why do people talk afterwards? No one should talk from Friday night to Sunday morning. The dark silence that the pastor drapes over their faces like deep hoods should stay with them until Easter morning sunlight blows it off. But it's "And how are your studies going?" "Gosh if I could sing as well as you do," "Oh excuse me a moment my diarrhea medicine hasn't yet kicked in." I don't answer anyone and think how much of a family do we have if my little smiles that stretch out flat are enough to fulfill my side of the conversation for them. Who forget that Jesus just did more than they will ever have the strength to.

Jesus gives his life and fills up the cup, the one that God wouldn't take, with blood. God brings him back but where's the miracle in that. He's God.

Coming back down just a little out of sight of camp, I smelled old flesh. A cloud of flies were swarming into and around the mangled body of a buck. It used to be huge, the pride of nature, but was ripped down into a thin nothing. I could see bite marks and the best hanks of flesh were missing. We hadn't heard the howls. Not this close. I bent into the gravel and poked at the prints I found there. There was no way of telling how many there were; enough at least to pound the level of the ground down an inch and a half. I left without making a cross because I couldn't set it on fire. An offering, burnt. Crosses burn to go to heaven. We jump and jump with our brains and legs but can't get higher than Mount Everest, not even with stilts. Burn us and we make it there on the devastating beauty of smoke and sparks. Brat was there. Dad was there and here. And Brat is here. I don't

137

care what his eyes say around the edges where emotion comes through: the color is his.

Grant was awake when I got back to camp. Dad and Mom were twined at the hands, asleep. I kicked pebbles not far enough to wake them. Grant fumbled over to the backpack and dug around inside it.

"We need more water," he said, pulling out empty bottles.

"Didn't think to make some nano for that, did you?"

"I did. I didn't bring it."

"We could send the lovebirds out for it. Which reminds me. Saw a mutilated deer up there a ways. Looks like the dogs got to it."

"Dogs? Not coyotes or cougars?"

"The pattern of bite marks was consistent with how the hell should I know?"

He set the bottles up in a row. Eight needed filling and a ninth was half empty. That left three still full. His eyes were careful.

"We don't absolutely need it, I guess."

"Thinking we need to stay together if the dogs come back?"

"Something like that."

"I'll turn them into bread."

His laugh was short, like a cough or a bark. Mom and Brat groaned in the same voice and opened their eyes. I threw one of the empty bottles at Brat. He fended it off with a groggy hand and tried to get me to scratch his back.

"It's broad daylight. Mom and Dad can go find some more water and we can scout ahead," I suggested.

"What if Brandt has another episode?"

"Then Mom can take care of him. She's a nurse."

"No she isn't."

"Well, if she was she would be. Look. We can find the easiest path for him. Save us problems once we start moving again."

"I was thinking about that, Lith. Maybe we should

head back."

"No." I didn't want to say more. He asked for reasons and I didn't give them. The town was gray to me and I wouldn't set my clean foot on it again. The town was a hypocrite lit by street lamps. I wouldn't touch her with my jagged finger nail. He asked. I didn't answer and he wouldn't leave without me.

I spilled a little water on Brat's groaning body. He scowled at me and tried to be stern, but his eyes weren't tired enough. A raven and his bullies broke through the muffling sunlight as they flew overhead.

"We need more water, Mom," I said. "Grunt and I are going to find the easiest route for you and—" I gestured. Dad, whose nose was bleeding. I reached down to touch it. He pulled away, stretching his own fingers up. They came away red and he tasted them. His skin was a pale yellow. It was time to hold a funeral.

"You can handle it, Dad?" asked Grant, bending over. I could see Brandt's wish to pull himself up to his full height though it wouldn't have done any good.

Mom was rising, sleep draining from her yawning mouth. "We can handle it." The yawn dropped her an octave. "Can't we darling?" Dad nodded. I could hear his teeth grinding as he tried not to let them chatter. To warm himself in Mom's smile, he said, "I missed you."

"Better take the blanket," I told him.

"Didn't do much last night. Why should it this morning," he grumbled but kept it around his shoulders.

"Head down the valley, I think," said Grant.

"I can tell, son."

"We'll go up."

"I don't like being babied," he slurred at Mom. She patted him on the shoulder and put bottles in his arms. We left them then, Dad spilling his guts. I hoped he would talk to her as he wouldn't have before. Open his teeth as though they were a gate and let the feelings run free.

"What happened to the mill?" I heard last in his

youngest son's voice. It should have been shuddering terror at losing first a year and a job, then a world. A body. A face that God remembered because he saw it holding back screams as Dad held a dirty rag over his mangled fingers from that one moment of carelessness with a saw. If I had been Dad resurrected, I would have moved my hands; I could have never stopped.

The jealousy gives out when Mom lays the bundle on the hard wood floor Daddy had me ripping all day. I helped the most of anyone. More than Grant. More than Daddy with my hammer with the claw coming out of its back.

Mom unfolds the thing that is meowing. It only has gums. That must be why it can't speak words.

"What's that?"

"That's where his umbilical cord was, honey. That's the piece that connects the baby to Mommy while it's inside of her."

"It looks like vegetable soup."

His face is so pink and pale at the same time. The claw on the end of my hammer could change him, so I had better not. He stops yowling to suck on Daddy's good fingers. He doesn't smell at all like vegetable soup.

"Where are you going?" asked Grant.

"I was going further up. I want a better view," I told him, spreading open my arms to embrace the beautiful sagebrush.

"You know, Lith, it might be helpful if, now that we're out of earshot, you were a little less antagonistic toward Dad. It'll make the transition smoother."

"It'll make him feel like he's died and gone to heaven."

"This is anything but."

"Oh come on," I said, putting one foot in front of another on higher ground. "No one to bother you, loving family, wife with her strong, square jaw on the ground, healthy young body, the natural stimuli of the great outdoors." I stripped a clump of whitish-gray foliage from a bush and held it to my nose. "They say the smell of decay is a natural aphrodisiac."

"Not a lot of privacy for them, here," said Grant. "You can't put a door just anywhere." He looked up the valley as far as his short eyes could stretch. "We should stay on this path for a ways."

"Go ahead."

"And we need to stick together."

"Shouldn't be too hard. I can't seem to get away from you. Your smell, anyway. You haven't showered since we left."

"You haven't."

"Yes, but I've got pheromones. Not bee-oh."

"Shut up and get down here."

I took another couple steps up the steeper side. No sudden hiss of a rattlesnake, slow in the sun, slow in the middle but not at each end. "No, I have the food. This time you follow me."

"Shit."

"Not on command."

"We forgot to feed Dad."

"He could live off tree bark for a week. The only human in history to have a working appendix."

He glanced up the valley again and was babysitting me when I was three years old.

"Okay. We cover more ground."

"I'll have the better view. Go on away. Your armpits will be with me forever." Like wood smoke and sweat; like bread. I fluttered my eyelashes at him. He wavered back and forth in the promising morning heat, as he was only air, then turned on both heels as on an axis and shut up. I dug my toes into the dust and went up.

This mountain had a name. It was taller than mine, but its base grew from higher and that was cheating. It was of sliced granite and piles of its children. I learned a long time ago that the old rock slides are about the easiest places to climb up. You can leap from spike to spire on invulnerable feet like a mountain goat which means you have cloven hooves.

At the frozen heart of the largest slide, I found a place where I could peer around the mountain's shoulder. Rows of purpling ridges grinned back at me, each higher than the last. It was like the optical illusion where water runs uphill forever; the mountains, the bones of the world, would each grow higher than the last, I knew, until they had fenced in the world clear around and came again to my ridge, the tallest of all in the end.

I blinked. Her drowned eyes. The Brat's face yellow and sick when it should have been gray and bloated or pink and white. I took off my shirt and cleared my eyes. A bee buzzed past, pausing at my left elbow on the faintest whiff of a scent, as it must have learned to do. Take anything small and build with it; take everything large you can find. He flew on. I started to praise God for the creatures small enough to survive. The thought was too big for me and was stillborn.

"Lith!" he called. That's why I turned, I swear. My foot slipped just a little, the distance of my smallest crooked toe. He yelled something else and the shoving waves of sound knocked me over without meaning anything. I fell back hard on my spine and blew out my air before it had the chance to cushion me. I heard a rumble deep in the pregnant belly of the mountain, so heavy it would have sunk beneath the Earth's crust if not for the ringing sky hooks of pebbles, fiercely crashing together like cymbals misplaced at the end of a funeral dirge. Skittering over the top of the rhythm.

My body was waving. The ground wasn't solid under my shoulder blades where I feel it the most. Grant yelled again; he must have been facing the other way because the sound spun around the world and caught me in the back of the neck, grinding me onto my feet.

I couldn't see and I could barely feel. Brown dust mixed with gray stones in the air. I had to breathe it. I hadn't a choice. I yelled things like "never never no" from the deepest parts of my cloaked lungs. Alone, I had to stumble down the mountainside to make it to the bottom alive. Standing still is suicide. I didn't think at the time.

I was at the bottom long after I knew I should have been. Watch out for the still loose and shifting rocks. A rigid fist, a four-fingered stone caught me, threw me, made something new in my ankle and I limped to where I thought his shirt would stick up like a flag for me to see.

"Grant!" Didn't answer. My heart beat harder than yours. But there was his shirt, half-invisible under a splintered boulder and I didn't think until then that I had forgotten which shirt he was wearing. I slapped him in the face and for a moment imagined that I hadn't found him, that this wasn't just a nightmare someone else was dreaming on me. Then he bled. I couldn't understand a word he was saying. It bubbled, the thought he tried to give me. I sagged off my legs, the twisted ankle crying and sucking its thumb. The dust was settling around us.

He was half on his stomach, caught from behind. What eyes he had were turning gray. I didn't mean it. I told him, so close to his ear the words couldn't miss. He spat.

"There is nothing wrong." He spat too much. "Stone. You, stone."

"I'm here. I'm your brother."

"I don't want to die in their jaws." Terror made him stronger. His eyes were closed; they made him stronger. "Maybe my soul can't leave if I'm in their jaws."

I was afraid my words were too clogged with dirt for him to understand. "I thought you didn't believe in a soul."

"I'm crying from my chemicals." He never would give me the satisfying slam of a museum gate closed safely. I can't get the satisfying slam of a heavy hard back, where the last word takes all its brothers and cups them in the evaporating bath of its cool black ink.

"Lith'm," I heard. My hand was on his throat so I wouldn't have to see the pulse of blood. He couldn't see. "Kill me. Nowever."

"Don't open—" your mouth because I don't want to hear the last of your thoughts as words I have spent so long with words I couldn't bear them anymore as you the last of you so dusty and over used.

"Please. Their jaws are sick." What could be so terrible as to make a grown man beg for an insult and broken unspoken rule to seem so much like the hand of God.

I took his head in my hands and left streaks on his face. I bent and kissed him on the lips, tasted only myself. He pleaded with me, thinking I wasn't going to help him escape. With Mom he could but Mom doesn't enter into this. This is my older brother, this is my older brother pouring something out his eyes like hatred at a world too stupid to see how small it is to slaughter its children and suffocate the survivors.

"Don't be the same," he said strong but coughing.

"I love—" you forever. I twisted his neck as hard as I could and felt an ugly snap and bump grow under my fingers. I fell back. Couldn't stand. Foot was broken or sprained.

How many before have died exactly as he did? We used to play a game on the bus. In the middle of our conversations, one or the other of us would stop and wonder aloud, "Do you think that anyone else in the world is having this same talk right now, right anywhere?" We never found one that felt too special to have come from any other tongues. We were just playing a tune.

I stood on top of the pain as a fire underneath me. I took off my shorts, slowly, and stood naked in front of his glued eyes. In the horizon, a dog howled. My bladder was hot and hurting. It was all I had, so I let it out instead of a scream. My penis flared and was as red as an infection. The dust puffed tiny clouds where my urine hit. I still felt the same. I sat down on a rock, spent. My ankle was bleeding.

I crawled, still naked, to find a stick I could use to support my weight. The one I found gave out halfway to camp. I hopped and hobbled as best I could after that and finally made it, dripping blood and snot. Mom and Dad were there, sipping water and holding their hands an inch apart.

Mom stood first and was going to ask me something and then her hands were up over her mouth not out. "What happened," through the net of her fingers.

"God damage." I cried. I vomited. And fell asleep.

Dad lost it. He slipped into a tirade that none of Mom's delicate glances could break him out of. I feared that he would get too big for his body, that he would become so swelled with his sense of injustice that the excess would come gushing out of the wrists that I doubted he had noticed yet. He threw stones at birds and swarmed around our small camp, bobbing the blanket back and forth across his shoulders like he couldn't bear either its weight or its absence. I shrank back against a scabby tree and nursed my ankle. He threw a rock at me which I dodged. He blamed me for moving and I took it; then he grabbed a black stick and stomped off, declaring that he was going to kill the goddamned beasts that took his son from him. "Gar," said Mom at last when it could do no good. She wanted to tell him it was already over and that it wasn't the dogs. It wouldn't have mattered, even if she could found the words. We heard him muttering a mile off. He would never find anything.

Mom's eyes pleaded with me to do something to fix her hurt. She had a hole that needed mending, and she believed that my explanation was the only tool that would meet. "Why?" she asked me more than once, and I with my unchanging and unsatisfying answer: because he asked me to. I told it to her a dozen different ways but it all meant the same to her. I was all she had left of her own blood, not even of her own name. She glared at me across the empty space in which a campfire should have been and I knew she saw a little of my Dad around the eyes. Brat looked more like her. In me she saw the second try, when she thought she could do better than Grant and found out she was wrong. After her error came her pink and pure boy and I, her mistake, gave thanks for every hurt that God blew in my way. She hated me for being in the middle of everything. Not frail enough to drown that one time in the lake, but not strong enough to swim ahead of her. Not handsome enough to get the girl, but not ugly enough to consign myself to a hermitage. Not independent enough to be Grant. Not grateful enough to be her baby. She hated me for being lukewarm and, like God, she spit me from her mouth without a second thought to argue with her first. Her life was a string of first thoughts acted upon: marriage, a child, a test, the third, and love again when the dead came walking, when her second thought should have been drenched in terror, swamped in bovine confusion.

But I'm wasting ink.

When I woke with the taste of something dead on my tongue, I was under the blanket and wearing the Brat's boxer shorts. A bottle of water was nearby. So was Dad. I rinsed my mouth out and gave him a heavy look, glancing down at my midsection after.

"Couldn't find your clothes. Your Mother thinks the dogs got to them." He paused. "They got to Grant. Et his face up pretty bad."

"It was pretty bad," I croaked.

"This was worse." He paused again. "So I gave you what I could."

"Where's Mom?"

"Off having a good cry." His lack of eyes told me what he didn't want to say, so I had an answer ready. Here came the question: "You did right, dear son."

"Because I—" wasn't ready for that. "What?"

He sighed, pulling the air in as I did with my eyes. "I never have to make that decision. I never had to think about pulling the plug on Grandpa. They didn't put him on life support. His request. But I thought about thinking about it, and it scared everything out of me. So much that at the funeral, I felt like I had killed him."

"Dad," I said after a long silence. "Why did you want us to burn you?" He felt my question for what it was: loose and flailing, like a whip, not a chain.

"You did it, did you? What was it like?"

"Hot. Smelly. We broke the fire code."

And then he wouldn't say anything else. He just waited for Mom to come back. When she did, I thanked God that at least he didn't have to go on tiptoes to kiss her.

I tried to staunch the blood from my ankle, pressing at the scrapes with a fistful of Witch's Hair moss. Mom saw me fumbling and came over to help. It hurt when she ground the moss over my skin, but I didn't say anything. If she needed to hurt me a little, I understood.

"I'm thinking." She hesitated. "Maybe we should go back."

I slapped a mosquito on my neck. "We don't know if it's safe yet, Mom."

"We didn't know it was dangerous, either. That was all Grant's idea."

Dad was flexing his fingers. He sighed at the air in his lungs: it wasn't his air, the kind he had when he was a kid. "If Grant thought it was a good idea, we should stick through it to the end."

"When is the end?" Mom asked.

"I think it happened," I tried to say, finding a new wash of phlegm and dust wiped across my tongue. Instead, it came out: "I think I'm in love."

I couldn't even have tried. What was left for me. The streets were empty except for the last day's trash and newspapers. I live in a house with the doors unhinged and piled in the closet. I don't, but there's no reason not to. Put out some dog food and watch old movies. Take the gas I want and host the Oscars, swept in a surprise upset by independent filmmaker Lithium for his faux-realist opus, "Etymology." The empty parties, the arguments. We wanted to fuck with archaeologists, so Grant and I buried tea cups next to porn engraved on metal siding. It was my idea. I can wait until I get senile and spend my summer days excavating our back yard, swallowing my dentures in surprise and embarrassed pleasure, avoiding Dad's grave, turning off my hearing aid so I can't hear Mom yelling at me to be careful.

"Lithium, honey? Could you make some bread? Your Father is getting hungry." Could she still starve to death? Or would her magic keep her holy, thin as a finger. A virgin again.

I twisted to grab a rock and pounded the ground, harder on each, like the stutters that build up to a scream. I didn't watch the dissolving. Right then it hurt, the thought of God playing at not noticing that I could take apart and rebuild his creation. I expected the weight to change.

"No," Grant would have said. "Law of Conservation of Mass." And thrown something at me. I ducked my head.

"Lith?"

"Mosquito." I handed Mom the bread. She tasted a bit and gave the rest to Dad.

"What'd we decide."

"We'll stay here until you can walk by yourself again," said Dad. "Then we'll head back. I wouldn't expect the military to stick around more than three days." It hadn't been only three days. It had been two almost three lifetimes which have to be longer than a day. The word is longer.

The words take so much longer. But do you know how many I can write in an hour? A bombed out week. I'm here, now, while they go off to fuck behind a rock. If we go home, I won't write anymore. Lying on the ground, on the pebbles, I can see where Brandt said goodbye and the other side of where Grant said to take him in my arms. Two straight lines piercing me as on a spit; the slow turning of the summer days are the fire, Dad's worthless funeral baking me into the ground. A feast forgotten, ruined on the stove.

"Dodo." There was a lot of affection throwing gravel across his whisper. The sun tripped over the mountain and went down. I lay transfixed by my brothers as Mom and Dad snuck behind a rock. Soon, their rhythmic scratching settled into white noise.

They wouldn't notice, so I scrambled to my feet,

scooping another large rock into my fist. I limped to a place where I could only see the stars through the lattice work of a cracked old tamarack. I brought down my hands, three times gently on my good ankle. Waited with my head up; the branches waved at me as though underwater and kissed by a smooth current. The wind carried a hint of the gray dust. I waved the bread under my nose when it was done.

With enough difficulty to be worth it, I crossed my legs. This is my body, broken for you. This is your body and I am going to break it in half, down the jagged center where not even you knew a fault lay. To become just a growth on the shoulder of the Earth; to become clean as from a burning cold hose. I was alone and ate the bread in the kind of sound I wished was silence; there were the air raid hums of mosquitoes, the chattering of thoughtless, angry squirrels; the howl of a dog who finds the sharp yellow stab of a scent he doesn't know; the susurration of my parents on the ground, louder, now, and as barren as the hiss of the rattlesnake I never saw. I am done. I licked my fingers. They tasted of rock, a brown taste.

I prayed again for rain and got nothing of the comfort I desired. The dogs were moving away, their cries less harsh and immediate. Perhaps they were hunting a bed of deer, or perhaps just chasing the moon like their big brothers. With them beyond the reach of my arms, the threat of the town seemed less, seemed more. Out in the wilderness, I have at least a direction, a path without a name that hasn't felt my feet before. Back there, I have a house with a carpet that is dimpled here and there exactly as a mirror to the shape of my heel and toes. I could move, once or twice. I could move every day. Eight billion people, at least three billion homes. I don't have that many days allotted me. When I was born, the doctor said three weeks and I am still holding him to it. Maybe I'll go live in a gay bar or something so unfamiliar. My eyes can't get used to neon advertising. It blinks on and off and it hums off and on and it is always the same as the last time until its brain stops and it goes dead.

I don't know the smell of alcohol well enough. It is the smell of the doctor's office, of pink plastic molding on the cold chairs and how come there's only old people when I go there with my need for surgery and everything sterile. I'm missing whole pieces of myself. The doctor and the beauty queen. I am missing these and I think that I missed myself to sleep.

It doesn't last long. My pen is starting to give up because I have pushed it too hard. Mom shook me a couple of minutes ago and took me by the chin.

"It's safe to go back."

"How do you know?"

"I did."

"You left us here?"

"After your Father went to sleep. He told me to. I wasn't tired. I was quick and careful and I knew you'd be okay. It's safe. I turned the air-conditioner on."

"What time is it?"

"The sun is up." It was. My tree was thick so I had to be thick, son. Be thick. "We're going home, now. Your Dad will carry you."

"He can't." Was I delirious, asleep. Something. Mom went behind the rock to wake him up. I won't write anymore not on paper, not imaginary things like this and that. It turns out not to matter, since my pen is almost out and we never lit a fire for the charcoal and burning hair.

I made breakfast and Dad has got the pack, bending him over just a little, only inches. Inches are so small. How could they matter?

He grinned at me.

Last ink. If you find this, burn it.

Printed in the United States
105605LV00004B/40-48/A